Juliette Hyland began crafting heroes and heroines in high school. She lives in Ohio, USA, with her Prince Charming, who has patiently listened to many rants regarding characters failing to follow their outline. When not working on fun and flirty happily-ever-afters, Juliette can be found spending time with her beautiful daughters, giant dogs, or sewing uneven stitches with her sewing machine.

Unlocking the Ex-Army Doc's Heart
is **Juliette Hyland**'s debut title

Look out for more books
from Juliette Hyland
Coming soon

Discover more at millsandboon.co.uk.

UNLOCKING THE EX-ARMY DOC'S HEART

JULIETTE HYLAND

MILLS & BOON

First published in Great Britain 2020
by Mills & Boon, an imprint of HarperCollins*Publishers*
1 London Bridge Street, London, SE1 9GF

Large Print edition 2020

© 2020 Juliette Hyland

ISBN: 978-0-263-08597-6

MIX
Paper from
responsible sources
FSC® C007454

This book is produced from independently certified
FSC™ paper to ensure responsible forest management. For
more information visit www.harpercollins.co.uk/green.

Printed and bound in Great Britain
by CPI Group (UK) Ltd, Croydon, CR0 4YY

For my husband,
who always believed my stories
would land on readers' bookshelves.

CHAPTER ONE

DR. RAFE BRADSTONE shivered as he stepped to the door of the small plane. Pulling his scarf across his mouth, he bounced from foot to foot as he grabbed his duffel bag. The wind blasted his face as he stepped onto the Tarmac, and goose bumps rose across his body. The heavy jacket he'd acquired at the last minute in LA seemed pathetically inadequate. How did the residents of the Arctic get warm?

Stepping into the airport waiting area, Rafe sighed as warm air slid around him.

"Excuse me." A woman with black curls pushed past him.

"Sorry, I didn't mean to stop in front of the door."

She didn't hear him as she raced toward a pair of happy kids. The kids hopped around her, each trying to outshout the other as their father hugged her. The love pooling between the small family was evident—these children never had to fight for their mother's attention.

Rafe's stomach tightened and he forced his eyes away from the lovely scene. It had been over a year since he'd found his mother, and two hundred and sixty-one days since she'd ordered him off her porch. Rafe wanted to believe the pain of her abandonment would fade, but his heart was still raw.

The woman with dark curls placed one child on her hip and held the other's hand as she walked out of the airport. That was the way it was supposed to be: a mother loved her children, wanted to be with them. Glaring at his hands, Rafe wondered why *his* mother didn't react that way. What was wrong with him that his simple presence caused her pain rather than excitement?

His phone beeped. Burying the pain, he answered without looking at the caller ID. "Hello, Carrie."

His agent didn't waste words on a greeting. "Why are there social media posts of you in Alaska?"

Rafe started to roll his eyes but caught himself. Carrie was *supposed* to be interested in his professional life. It wasn't her fault this opportunity for him to serve in Blue Ash, Alaska, conflicted with his television duties, or that witnessing a family hugging their mom had put him in such a bad mood.

Keeping his tone level, he leaned against the wall. "Because I ran into a few fans of *The Dr. Dave Show*. They wanted a selfie, and I couldn't say no."

That wasn't true. He could have said no, but Rafe never wanted to. Whenever someone ran up to him, phone outstretched and excited, Rafe got to be a part of their life—to belong. It only lasted a moment, but he treasured each fan who wanted a memory with him. They never told him to go away.

Rafe had accepted the part-time host position on *Dr. Dave*, a medical talk show promoting healthy living techniques, hosted by a bevy of attractive practitioners, to help pay off his medical school debts. The legion of daytime television fans was just a great perk.

"You know that isn't what I mean." The sound of Carrie's nails clicking on her desk echoed down the phone.

Chuckling, Rafe ignored her tone. "I told you I was volunteering at an outpost clinic in Northern Alaska for a few weeks."

"I assumed you were *joking*." Her screech tore

through the speaker. "You're Dave's favorite substitute host, and you're scheduled to be on during the live Thanksgiving special!"

"I know my schedule."

His stomach hollowed, and a sigh escaped his lips. Volunteering for the Thanksgiving and Christmas episodes was supposed to make him forget there wasn't a chair waiting for him at anyone's table, though it never worked.

"Rafe! Are you even listening to me? This is serious."

"You're pretty hard to ignore."

Taking a deep breath, he stared out the window, letting his eyes roam the frozen landscape. Trees coated with icicles hugged the side of the airport, dropping loose snow along the cars in the parking lot.

Rafe shivered; he didn't belong in Alaska. In his experience winter meant a windbreaker or a light sweater, not parkas and boots. He might need to wear all his socks just to keep warm.

But his cold feet were tomorrow's obstacle. Sliding down the wall, Rafe tried to get comfortable while he tackled his current problem. "I am a doctor first, Carrie. Besides, I owe Dr. Freson."

Jenn had covered for him during his disastrous visit with his mom. She had never asked why he suddenly needed an extra two weeks of vacation, or why he'd come back with no fun stories or pictures. He owed her, and the possibility that Dave might need him wasn't a good enough reason for Rafe to refuse to help a friend.

"Today is the thirtieth of September. I'll be gone four weeks—six at the most. That puts me back in LA in plenty of time for Thanksgiving."

"Dave is looking to fill Dr. Bloom's spot at the end of the season, Rafe. That job should be yours. And rather than fighting for it you've disappeared."

Drumming his fingers on his knee, Rafe rolled his neck. He wanted that position. It wasn't the money or the fame. Rafe wanted Dave and the producers to choose him. For them to look at the other remarkable candidates and decide he was the best. Maybe that would quiet his mother's voice telling him he wasn't enough.

"There are other hosts; I need to do this."

Rafe frowned as Carrie sucked in a breath on the other end of the call.

"Rafe…" Carrie's voice shifted to the tone she used when letting her clients know they hadn't got a part. "Do you want me to issue a statement to the press? It isn't fair that the tabloids are accusing you of infidelity. Your reputation shouldn't be tarnished since Vanessa was the cheater."

He didn't want to discuss this topic either, but it was safer than worrying about Dave's penchant for firing hosts.

"Vanessa didn't cheat on me." The lie slid through Rafe's lips.

He'd met the movie star on the set of *Dr. Dave* six months ago. The paparazzi had loved getting pictures of the starlet and "her" doctor. She'd hidden her affair with another man—not that it had been hard to do. Their hectic schedules had resulted in more canceled plans than dates, but he'd assumed they were fine. She'd ended it over the phone while she giggled with her co-star and lover.

He hadn't thought they needed to issue a public statement announcing their breakup. Vanessa had insisted. It had come as a nasty surprise when the tabloids had run a picture of him walking a patient to her car along with Vanessa's publicity statement saying that they had parted ways.

Seeing his name trending with "cheating" headlines had cut deeply. He'd bought every trashy magazine in the corner store by his apartment so he didn't have to see it. Rafe had always been faithful—*always*.

Vanessa could have corrected the assumption that he had cheated on her, accepted responsibility. He'd reached out to her a few times—unsuccessfully. If she hadn't corrected the story by now, she wasn't going to.

"My agent likes to remind me there's no such thing as bad press." Rafe blew onto his fingers.

Carrie clicked her tongue... "It does keep your name in the papers. Dave will like that."

Rafe pinched his nose. He wanted Dave to like his presence on set, his interview style, his high ratings—not his ability to land in the tabloids. Still, if that was what it took to land the gig, Rafe would accept the tabloid smear—even if he hated their falsehoods.

"I'll see you in a month."

Carrie's sighed. "A month is a long time in this town."

"And yet it's still only thirty days."

Static rose on the line, and Rafe shook his head. His agent wasn't great at goodbyes.

He smiled as a plump middle-aged woman rushed toward him. She danced on her toes while she waited for him to stand.

"Dr. Bradstone! It *is* you! I love *The Dr. Dave Show*. You should be on all the time. Your interviews are always the best. Better than Dave's! Can I get a picture with you?"

"Of course."

His soul felt a touch lighter as she slid her arm around his waist and his loneliness disappeared as she raised her cellphone. He owed this brief window of happiness to *The Dr. Dave Show*. Rafe was determined to get that fulltime host position and all the acceptance that came with it.

Patches of pink highlighted her cheeks as the woman stepped back. "Thank you." Pushing a strand of salt-and-pepper hair from her face, she scrunched her nose. "I'm Helen Henkle and this is my husband, Jack." She nodded toward a reed-thin man striding toward them. "We're your ride to Blue Ash."

Jack barely glanced at Rafe as he huffed, "You're going to need better shoes if you want to keep all of your appendages."

Variations on this theme had peppered Rafe's conversations since he'd crossed the Alaskan border yesterday. The tingle of cold in his toes made it seem more dire now that he was in the Arctic Circle.

Staring at his shoes, Rafe moved his digits. "We don't have much need for cold weather gear in Los Angeles."

"Well, up here it can mean the difference between ten toes or two. Don't want to explain to your grandchildren that you sacrificed a few toes rather than wear sensible boots."

Helen slapped her husband on the shoulder before offering Rafe a smile. "A man can get around on eight toes." Ignoring her husband's frown, Helen waved her hand toward Jack's feet. "It'll be a good way to ensure your children or grandchildren always wear their boots."

A flash of pain echoed across his belly as Rafe grabbed his bag and followed them onto the Tarmac. It didn't matter how many toes he kept, there were going to be no grandchildren to look at his feet. His family tree didn't have a great track record as parents, and Rafe didn't plan to extend that legacy.

Helen giggled as she slid into the seat next to him in Jack's tiny plane. "A real celebrity in Blue Ash. Well, if you don't count—" Helen coughed and smiled at her husband.

"Dr. A is expecting us. If you and the Playboy Doctor are ready, we'll get going."

Playboy Doctor... That tagline had been assigned to him because it sold magazines and received website clicks, not because it was true.

"That isn't a word I'd use to describe myself."

The defense slid from Rafe's lips before he could stop it. He didn't owe these strangers, or anyone else, an explanation.

"Of course." The words were even, but the man's lip twitched before he let his eyes slide over Rafe.

Rafe shifted, hating the ball of tension pooling in his belly. He'd been weighed and found lacking. *Again*... It shouldn't matter. Rafe didn't know Jack or Helen. Still his tongue itched to defend himself, to make them understand that Rafe knew what playboys were and how much damage they could cause.

After all, he looked just like a particular one—though the tabloids didn't know that. To them it was a flashy headline. To Rafe it was a curse.

Rafe was his father's doppelganger. His mother had referred to him as his father's mini-me—though it hadn't been a term of endearment. Rafe's father had been an attractive professional dancer, and he'd been on the road constantly. His mother's stable job as an accounting assistant had kept a roof over their heads, but with each new trip away for his father, each new booking, each lonely night, she'd become more vindictive.

When his parents hadn't been arguing about his father's many infidelities, they'd been yelling about Rafe. His mother would scream that she never got a break from being a mom—no fancy dancing getaways for her. His father would yell that he hadn't wanted a kid anyway.

Neither of them had paid any attention to the small child in the corner. Rafe might not have understood everything they were screaming about, but he'd always known that his father hadn't wanted him.

Why had he believed his mother had?

Rubbing his hands on his pants, Rafe tried to focus on the frozen scenery below. His father had died in a car accident with another woman a few days after his seventh birthday. A date neither of his parents had remembered, let alone celebrated. His mother had always constantly reminded Rafe of how he looked like the stupid cheater she'd married. She'd given up even trying to pretend she cared after that.

Infidelity had destroyed his family, and he would never repeat that mistake.

A few days before his eighth birthday, Social Services had taken custody of him. Rafe had bounced around the system until he'd aged out on his eighteenth birthday. He'd lived with many families but had never earned acceptance—never got to permanently *belong*. Now, when he was on set, he was the successful Dr. Rafe Bradstone, and for a little while that wound in his heart that had never closed bled a bit less.

Rafe was grateful no one attempted to make small talk on the short hop to Blue Ash. He needed to close off the pain twisting through him.

Rafe squinted as a small runway began to take shape ahead. "Are we going to land there?" The strip didn't look wide enough to handle the small Cessna.

Patting the plane's yoke, Jack grinned. "Don't worry, Doc. I've landed my baby in much worse conditions."

The broad smile spilling across Jack's craggy features did little to calm the nerves dancing in Rafe's belly. And as the wheels touched the ground they slid. Rafe's cry of alarm echoed through the tiny cockpit, but his fear was quickly replaced with embarrassment as Jack pulled the plane to a perfect stop.

"That runway has one patch of ice and you aimed for it. There was no need to demonstrate your skill on ice!" a husky voice yelled over the sound of the slowing propellers.

"Gotta toughen up the newbie. This region doesn't usually get stars whose faces are splashed across the tabloids." Jack tossed Rafe's bag to him as he turned to greet the young woman on the Tarmac.

"Tabloids are designed to make money, Jack, not to tell the truth."

The tiny welcome party was buried in an over-size parka, and her bright orange scarf hid everything but her stunning gray eyes. She met Rafe's gaze. The roar of the engine, the pilot's judgement, even the bite of the wind as it stole through his jacket—all vanished as her eyes searched his.

"I bet you're cold!" She motioned for him to follow her into what he assumed must be the clinic.

Heat marched up Rafe's neck. He hadn't even introduced himself—just stared at her. Matching her step, Rafe tried to think of a way to salvage this introduction.

"Welcome to Blue Ash."

Red hair tumbled from the hood of the parka as the woman hung her coat on a hook.

"Thanks."

Freckles danced across her nose, and Rafe sucked in a breath. His fingers wanted to trace each one. It was a ridiculous notion. She was exquisite, but so were many of the women in and around LA.

Fire erupted across his skin as he tried to regain his composure. He was *not* going to make a fool of himself. Rafe flashed a bright smile as he hung up his own coat. He would swear he knew her, but it was a crazy thought. Rafe didn't know anyone in this state. His brain itched, urging him to find her name.

His heart sped up as his mind put the puzzle pieces together. He barely resisted the urge to slap himself. This Arctic goddess was a woman he and much of the world had once welcomed into their living rooms weekly.

"You're Charlotte Greene."

"I played the *character* Charlotte Greene." The phrase didn't sound bitter as it escaped her lips, just resigned—and exceedingly well rehearsed. "My *name* is Annie…"

"Right…"

Everyone knew who Annie was; she'd graced every teen magazine and even landed a cover for *Vogue* before she turned seventeen. He hadn't meant to refer to her as Charlotte Greene. It had just popped out.

"I didn't realize you were hiding in Alaska."

Regret pooled around him as her full lips turned down. He was saying all the wrong things.

Annie crossed her arms as she lifted her chin. "I'm not hiding."

Rafe raised a brow but didn't argue. Dr. Freson had told him the Blue Ash Clinic was growing, but it served a community of less than six hundred. It was an odd place for the famous Annie Masters to put down roots.

"Your mom—"

Annie flinched as she interrupted him. "Carrie and I are not in regular contact. I cannot get you a meeting with her—and I doubt she represents television doctors."

Television doctors... Vanessa had made the same comment. Rafe might not win any awards for his work on *The Dr. Dave Show*, but the show helped people. He was more than a television doctor.

"I don't need an introduction."

Annie nodded, but Rafe doubted she believed him. She crossed her arms before offering him a tight smile.

But Rafe was not going to let the early stumble ruffle him. Smiling, he offered his hand. He always loved it when his fans talked to him about *Dr. Dave*. Annie probably didn't see many fans of *My Sister's House* in Blue Ash. Maybe if he flattered her work she'd relax a bit.

"I grew up watching *My Sister's House.* I've dreamed of meeting you since I was a kid."

Heat tore through him as she held his gaze again. Gold sparkled at the edge of her gray eyes as they traced his body. The camera had never caught that glimmer. *Annie Masters...* The intense connection Rafe had imagined on the runway bowled through him again.

"Nice to meet you, then, Dr. Bradstone."

Her cool tone rippled up his back. He was imagining their connection—just as he'd imagined a strong connection with Vanessa and his mother. He was not going to make that mistake again.

Sucking in a deep breath, Rafe straightened his shoulders. He didn't need to impress her. *He didn't...* He looked past her at the closed door to the back of the clinic.

Where was the doctor? He was supposed to be helping—not fumbling with words in front of a former starlet apparently now working as a receptionist in this remote Alaskan clinic.

Tipping his head toward the door, Rafe shrugged. "Is Dr. A with a patient?" He hoped his use of the nickname Jack had used for the doctor might lighten the uncomfortable mood in the small reception area.

"It's Dr. Masters. Only my patients call me Dr. A."

Annie's sharp response slapped him.

"*Dr.* Annie Masters."

She raised her chin, daring him to ask how a child star had landed in this position—here.

His stomach lurched as his brain searched for words. "Dr. Freson failed to mention…"

Annie let out a soft chuckle, before shifting back on her heels. "Well, Jenn does have a wicked sense of humor."

"We need to get going." The awkwardness in Helen Henkle's statement carried across the room. She offered Rafe an uncertain smile as she continued. "If you need more supplies let us know, Annie. We probably only have a few more weeks of easy flights."

Rafe hadn't realized they'd followed them into the clinic. Rafe wondered if his star had faded a bit in Helen's eyes now she'd witnessed this interaction. Then her final words registered against his cluttered brain. "Wait—what do you mean only a few more weeks?"

"Winter sets in early. If you aren't out of here by the third week of November you might have to stay until mid-March, Dr. Bradstone."

Annie Masters leaned against the reception

desk, the corner of her lip twisted in what he thought was a smile. Was she challenging him? He *couldn't* stay through the winter. He'd be in breach of contract if he missed the Thanksgiving and Christmas episodes of *Dr. Dave*.

"I have to be back in LA by the last week of November."

Annie—*Dr. Masters*—nodded. "You should be fine. The worst of the winter is still weeks away." Her hand ran along the torn skin of her thumb before she shrugged. "If you're worried you don't have to stay. Jenn will be here before winter really sets in."

"And if she's not?"

Annie's shoulders tensed and her fingers trembled, but her face remained still. "I've handled four lone winters. It's—" Again Annie pulled at the skin along her thumb. "I'm used to being by myself."

Shifting on his feet, Rafe fiddled with the strap of his bag. "Lone?" Why did that worry him? Clearly she'd managed.

She shrugged, and Rafe's heart ached. Loneliness was apparently Annie's constant companion too. He'd learned to accept its presence after his mother's abandonment—why had a popular child star been forced to learn the same lesson?

Annie gestured toward the door leading to the back of the clinic. "*If* you're staying, your apartment is this way."

She turned and walked through a side door. She left it standing open, but didn't wait for him. This was a challenge—a test. She expected an LA television doctor to at least consider fleeing.

But Rafe was not going to be underestimated by Dr. Annie Masters. Hiking his bag up his shoulder, Rafe took off after her.

Annie hustled past exam rooms as she hurried toward the stairs leading to her apartment at the back of her clinic. She knew Rafe—*Dr. Bradstone*—would follow. The man was too cocky to flee—even if he wasn't cut out for the Arctic. His jacket and shoes wouldn't protect him. The clinic was on the edge of the Arctic Circle. By the end of next month it would be dangerous to be outside for more than a few minutes, even with proper winter gear. This life was not for everyone.

Still, when he'd landed she'd felt—

Annie bit her lip as she tried to understand why they'd stood on the runway staring at each other.

In that moment she'd felt warm, despite the chilly wind pushing against them. Her heart had sped up as if it was trying to escape her chest, though she doubted he'd noticed.

Rafe Bradstone was used to attention—lots of it. He was an excellent general practitioner—one of the best in LA. And his ties to the entertainment industry ensured anyone watching *The Dr. Dave Show* knew he was both skilled and gorgeous. He was constantly reaching out to his fans—and they seemed to be everywhere.

The clinic had fielded more appointment calls this week than it had for the last two months. Everyone wanted to see Dr. Bradstone. This was going to be her life for as long as Rafe was in residence. The man was a distraction—an exceptionally attractive distraction.

Why had Jenn sent Rafe as a temporary replacement? Annie had met her best friend on the first day of medical school. She'd been the only one to introduce herself and keep their conversation focused away from Annie's days on set. Her friend was passionate about medical access for all, and she'd promised Annie the best replacement doctor for her clinic.

Maybe she should have asked for the second-best.

Annie clenched her fists as the selfish thought slid through her. Her patients weren't as glamorous as the ones Dr. Bradstone usually treated, but they deserved the best. It wasn't their fault Rafe had used his medical knowledge, self-assurance and good looks as a path to celebrity.

Blue Ash had seen a population boom since Rickon Oil had announced it was opening a satellite location just outside of the town. The clinic needed two doctors to see to the expanding list of patients. Finding a doctor willing to spend the winter in near darkness, with temperatures south of negative twenty degrees, wasn't easy. Her last new hire had left her in the lurch, with winter quickly approaching. So when Jenn had offered to spend the winter with her in Blue Ash, Annie had quickly accepted.

Her friend had sworn that Rafe would help until the middle of November, and promised she'd be here by then. But what if Jenn decided she needed to stay in LA after she moved her father into his retirement home and Rafe left?

Swallowing the fear racing up her throat, Annie straightened her shoulders. She had overstated her confidence in spending the winter alone, but if she had to she would serve the community alone for another winter.

Passing the rows of silly photos and artwork her patients created, Annie resisted the urge to turn and gauge Rafe's reaction. His office in LA was probably professionally decorated, but she loved her homey clinic. It didn't matter what a celebrity doctor thought of her space—he was just a temporary Arctic resident.

When she'd first opened up, one of her young patients had painted a picture of Annie and her clinic. Annie was only recognizable by the crazy red curls on the stick figure's head, and the clinic was an amorphous blob, but little Nicole had been so proud when Annie had placed it on the wall. And over the last several years the clinic had become a miniature art and photography gallery.

Walking up the stairs and pausing at the apartment door, Annie took a deep breath before turning around. Rafe was several steps behind her. Tipping her head, Annie pursed her lips. What was *wrong* with her? She'd dared him to leave. Not a good way to welcome the new doctor—even if he *was* an arrogant celebrity physician who'd called her Charlotte Greene.

That was a name that belonged to another lifetime, but Rafe wasn't the first to call her by name of the character she'd played from the age of seven to eighteen. Still, it hurt that the first name out of this stunning man's full, wind-chapped lips hadn't been Annie.

Even after all these years away from the spotlight, the role her mother had secured for her daughter still haunted her. Carrie had managed Annie's career right from her first commercial, and she'd had no plans to give up her position when her daughter had stepped into adulthood. So, in order to "help" Annie transition from child actress to adult superstar, Annie's mother had sold pictures of her daughter sunbathing topless.

The story that went with them hadn't talked about how Carrie had practically forced Annie onto the secluded "private" beach and criticized her tan lines until Annie had finally slipped off the bikini top. It had simply run with the headline *Child Star All Grown Up—New Roles Pouring in for Annie Masters.*

It had been the final straw. She'd known she had to do something—anything—to escape Carrie's control.

And at eighteen she'd marched away from her mother and from Hollywood—literally. She'd walked into an Army recruiting office during her mother's hair appointment and signed enlistment papers. The Army had been supposed to be Annie's escape—instead she'd found her purpose, first as an Army medic and then as a doctor.

But stepping away from Hollywood hadn't been easy. Annie had fought constantly to be taken seriously. She'd focused on proving herself in the field. Making friends had taken even longer. For a long time Annie hadn't been allowed to have any privacy without being called a snob, or worse. She'd hated it that everyone had expected the bubbly, personable Charlotte Greene. It had been almost as if she'd failed them by not meeting their expectations—particularly men. A lot of them had grown up watching her—fantasizing about her.

Except it hadn't been *Annie* any of them had wanted. In the decade since she'd left Charlotte Greene behind, only one man had seen past the character, and now he was gone too.

"I'm sorry. It was unfair to assume you weren't the doctor here." Rafe leaned against the wall, and ran his hand over his face. "And I apologize for calling you Charlotte Greene. I look forward to working with you, Dr. Masters."

His apology stole a bit of Annie's fire. And his reaction was normal—perhaps that was why it hurt so much. Maybe she still hoped to find someone who'd want Annie, not the character projected on a TV screen.

The role of Charlotte had given her financial independence, but how did you measure the cost of loneliness?

Wrapping her arms around herself, she nodded. Swallowing her pride, she offered a hand. "Want to start over?"

"Yes—but can you answer one question?"

"Ask away." She braced herself for some inane question about Hollywood, or the show she'd worked on. It wasn't his fault; it was what everyone wanted from her.

"Why am I still cold? I can feel the heat, but I swear my body refuses to accept it."

A pool of happiness opened inside her as his dark eyes held hers. Rafe wasn't going to press her for any Hollywood details. It was a simple gesture, but she appreciated it.

"Southerners can be so weak." A small giggle escaped her lips. "It's because your feet are damp. The rest of your body is trying to compensate."

Resting his large hands on his hips, Rafe chuckled. "I don't think California really counts as the south."

The rich baritone of his chuckle filled the

room, rushing through her body. Tingles raced down her spine and blood pounded through Annie's ears.

Trying to ignore the unexpected uptick in her heartbeat, Annie shrugged. "Anything south of the Alaskan border is the south."

How did anyone concentrate around this gorgeous man? Rafe was stunning! She hadn't found anyone so attractive since Blake.

Her fiancé had been gone for years, but she'd kept a few of his things. During her first two winters in Blue Ash, Annie had worn Blake's sweaters, and silly wool socks, not caring that they were four sizes too big for her. They were ridiculous items to keep, but donating them hadn't seemed like an option.

Last winter she'd pulled them out but hadn't worn any of them. Maybe it was time to finally clear out the drawers. Blake...

"Annie?"

Shaking herself free from the past, Annie took a step back. She needed to put a bit of distance between them. "Sorry, what did you say?"

Rafe moved closer, but he didn't crowd her. "I said, aren't you from California too?"

"Yes."

Sandalwood and lemon erupted across her

senses. Of *course* Rafe would smell as good as he looked.

Annie gestured to her own feet. "And it took three winters before people stopped telling me all the different ways I was likely to lose my toes. Although I feel honor bound to warn you—"

"My shoes aren't made for winter. Several individuals have already informed me. So, in three winters I'll be a regular Alaskan—assuming I upgrade my footgear?" He laughed as he spun around her small kitchen.

"Your Arctic experience so far already has you thinking of becoming one of us?"

Annie pursed her lips, unwilling to admit to the leap of fire darting across her belly. It would be nice to pretend someone else would land in Blue Ash and see it the way she did—recognize it as home. But that was not going to be Dr. Bradstone. He wanted spotlights and a fan base—not long winters and nightless summers.

"Is there a place to set this down or am I sleeping in the kitchen?" Rafe let out an uncomfortable laugh. "I fear it's been a while since I slept on the floor, but I can manage."

Annie motioned for him to follow her to the guest room. "Do you enjoy camping?" She'd slept on the ground many times during her Army service and didn't particularly like it.

"No." Rafe's voice was strained as he laid his bag on the bed and began digging through it.

"Then why did you sleep on the floor? Was it a silly kids' game?" Annie had worked all through her childhood, but she was always fascinated to hear about the imaginary games other kids had played to occupy their time.

"Didn't always have a bed." Rafe's words were clipped.

Why hadn't he had a bed?

Rafe didn't elaborate as he grabbed another pair of socks.

Swallowing the questions stuck in her throat, Annie frowned at the thin socks in his hands. "You're in the Arctic, Dr. Bradstone. You *will* lose your toes if you wear those."

She turned to the closet. He might enjoy the trappings of celebrity, but she didn't want him to suffer under her roof.

"Here."

She tossed a pair of Blake's thick wool socks to Rafe. Rafe pulled them on and sighed—just like Blake used to. She had always joked that her fiancé loved putting on socks more than anything else.

Annie's heart clenched as Rafe slid his feet into the pair of boots she'd given him. Rafe wasn't Blake. He was attractive, and she didn't want him losing any toes on her watch. That was it.

"Do all Arctic residents maintain a supply of socks for us weak southerners?" Rafe smiled as he stood.

"No." The bell at the front of her apartment saved Annie from finding a reason for the socks. She didn't talk about Blake—ever.

"Dr. A? We need you."

A scream echoed up the hall as she raced for the front of the clinic, Rafe close behind her.

She saw Danny Mills' eyes dart quickly to the newcomer before shifting back to Annie. "I was moving some of the food drums for the animals and one fell. I didn't—"

"Who's hurt and where?" Annie interrupted as she looked behind him. She'd talk to Danny about the accident later—now she needed facts.

Danny's lower lip trembled. "Grandpa Mac. He tried to catch the drum, but it landed on his leg. It's bleeding—bad. Jeremiah's bringing him in now."

Before Annie could say anything, Rafe rushed for the door—without his coat.

"Not a smart move…" Danny's whispered

words held a faint hint of admiration as the door slammed shut.

Annie sighed. Rafe's decision was foolish. It was just the sort of showboating one might expect of a doctor on a television show. Still, she admired Rafe's dedication.

"Direct them into Room Three, Danny. I'm going to grab supplies."

Annie maintained only a small supply of blood. She knew Mac was O positive, but she quickly double-checked his chart. Any injury was going to slow him down heading into winter preparations. And the older man would refuse to take any days of vacation or rest. She mentally ran through a few arguments that might convince the hard worker to let his legion of children and grandkids do the heavy lifting for a week or so. Maybe Rafe could try his hand.

Another scream tore through the clinic, and Annie's fingers fumbled with the stitches she was laying out. Mac's pain tolerance was legendary. And people often overestimated the amount of blood their loved ones had lost. But what if Danny hadn't?

"Annie!"

Rafe's call sent shivers of fear down her spine as she grabbed the blood and ran from the room.

"What's...?" The word died on her lips as she stumbled into Room Three.

Mac's face was ashen. A jagged cut ran from his ankle to just below his knee, but the bone wasn't visible in the coating of blood. That was good.

"How much of this is dried blood?" Annie pushed past Danny and Jeremiah, deposited the blood bag on a hook and moved to Rafe's side.

The wound needed to be cleaned, and it was going to require at least two dozen stitches. It was a simple fix, but with the amount of blood he'd lost...

Annie let those thoughts slide away as she looked to Rafe.

"Most of it—but there is still one bleeder up by the knee."

"What's that mean?" Danny's frightened voice swelled through the room.

"It means I need Dr. A's help to treat your grandfather." Rafe nodded to the teenager. "Can you and Jeremiah go get your grandmother?"

Danny's face lit up with relief and purpose as he pushed toward the door. "We'll be back real soon."

She shot a quick smile at Rafe. Mac's grandsons were too antsy to be allowed to stay, but

Rafe had given them a job to complete rather than an order to vacate the room. It had been the right move, and Annie was grateful.

Turning her attention to Mac, Annie stepped up next to the bed. "We need to clean the wound, Mac, so Dr. Bradstone and I can get a better look. Then I think it's best if we move you into the operating theater. You're going to need a number of stitches and the light is better in there."

"You sure? Maybe just a Band-Aid?" Mac offered a soft smile as he grimaced.

"It's good you're still making jokes." Rafe winked at Mac before turning to Annie. "What would you like me to do? Clean or suture?"

Mac gripped Annie's hand. "Stay with me."

"Looks like you're suturing." Annie smiled at Mac before looking up to Rafe. "The sutures are laid out in the theater—it's the second to last door on the right."

Rafe nodded as he headed to the door. "I'll go get everything ready. I still can't believe I'm working with…" The words faded as Rafe disappeared through the door.

Unfortunately Annie's mind had no trouble supplying them. Everyone always wanted Charlotte Greene.

But Rafe was a temporary clinician—a man

who wanted the fancy lights of Tinseltown. It didn't matter that he wished she was someone else.

It didn't.

CHAPTER TWO

ANNIE'S EYES WIDENED as she wheeled Mac into the small operating theater, but she didn't laugh at Rafe's attire.

Their patient didn't hold back, though. "Quite the outfit, Doc!"

He'd found a pair of floral scrubs in the scrub room. They fit his waist, but his calves were still visible. Unfortunately, none of Annie's scrub tops would get past his shoulders. His clean white T-shirt left little to the imagination.

Rafe pressed his lips together as Annie's eyes wandered over his outfit. He didn't look like a fancy television doctor *now*.

Her eyes finally darted to his and her lips twitched. Then, glancing at Mac, Annie headed for the door. "I delivered the local anesthetic three minutes ago. I should wash up again."

Her shoulders bounced with laughter as she bolted.

Mac's hands lay across his stomach, and his breath came in even pulses.

"I assume, since you laughed at my scrubs, that the numbing agent Dr. Masters has administered is working?"

"I can't feel the injury."

Mac nodded, but his eyes hovered over Rafe's feet. And the older man's fingers twitched as he refused to meet Rafe's gaze. Was he trying to hide his pain?

"Mac, if you're not numb I need you to tell me. Stitching the wound is going to take some time, and I don't want to hurt you."

Mac's eyes finally met his. "I'm numb. I'm just embarrassed. When Dr. A. gave me those shots…" His cheeks flamed as he closed his eyes. "It burned like hell and I yelled at her."

Pain was a great equalizer.

Offering Mac a soft smile, Rafe tried to soothe his worry. "Lidocaine often burns. There's no shame in admitting to pain. I'm sure Dr. A didn't mind."

Rafe picked up the sutures and began working his way up Mac's leg.

"Of course not." Annie smiled as the door slid closed behind her. "I've had Army Rangers scream expletives that would turn your ears pink

as I treated them. They used much more color-
ful terms than you did, Mac. I thought no less
of them, and I think no less of you."

Annie nodded to Rafe as she took her place on
the opposite side of the table.

"I think you'll need to stay tonight for obser-
vation," she told Mac.

Mac frowned. "Not that I'd mind spending the
night with you, Doc, but my bed is more comfortable."

"Why, Mac! Are you flirting with me?" Annie
pretended to flip her hair back as she looked at
Rafe's sutures. "What would Molly think?"

"She'd tell me I could do no better than Dr. A
but she'd shoot me if I tried."

"My heart flutters!" Annie laughed. "Tell me
about your new great-grand-baby."

Annie smiled as she listened to Mac discuss
the joys of family life. The older man's family
sounded chaotic, loud and perfect. Rafe's chest
tightened as the happy stories floated around the
room. He would have loved to belong to a family like Mac's. It sounded like there would be a
large cadre of caretakers while Mac healed. Rafe
hoped his family knew how lucky they were.

Taking a deep breath, Rafe let the world narrow to Mac's leg as he continued pulling the skin

together. He'd already placed twenty stitches and had at least another twenty more to go. Mac's scar was going to be epic.

"Done." Rafe enjoyed the look of shock on Mac's face.

"Thought you were just getting started." The older man looked at the wound and paled.

Reacting fast, Annie put her hands under Mac's neck and gently lay him back on the table. "You lost a decent amount of blood and that wound is going to be tender for several weeks. We're going to get you back to your room and give you something to help you sleep."

Rafe frowned. Annie was an excellent doctor. She could practice anywhere. Why was she hiding in an outpost clinic in the frozen Arctic?

Mac's eyes bounced back to the wound before landing on the ceiling. He pursed his lips but managed a small whistle. "Going to be quite the scar."

"I did my best to minimize it, but the scar will be noticeable." He'd seen more than one patient tear up over a scar, though Rafe was surprised it bothered this hardened Alaskan. "Plastic surgery once it has healed might be an option—"

Mac waved his hand. "It's not my beautiful figure I'm worried about, Doc. It's my pride—I need to figure out a better story than being attacked by a food drum."

Rafe laughed. "Are there mountain lions in this area?" he asked.

Heat pooled along his neck as Annie and Mac looked at each other, clearly amused by the question.

"No mountain lions for a couple hundred miles, son." Mac's lips pulled to one side, but he didn't actually laugh.

Trying to salvage his own pride, Rafe asked, "What about bears?"

And at least neither of them dismissed that idea as they transferred Mac back to his room.

Mac's breathing slowed as the pain medication took effect.

"Where did you treat Army Rangers?" The question tumbled from Rafe's lips into the room as Mac's first snores started.

"In the Army." Annie gestured for him to follow her.

"I'm serious, Dr. Masters."

Annie shook her head. "I've been many things since I was Charlotte Greene. She's what people want to know about, but I served as a combat medic for four years before going to med school, Dr. Bradstone."

Rafe tried to picture the woman before him in fatigues. The image came much more easily than he'd anticipated.

"A combat medic?"

Awe spread through him. He had seen a lot of trauma during his emergency room rotations, and a few of those days were burned into his memory. He could only imagine Annie's experiences.

"I'd say you're a lot more than Charlotte Greene."

Annie offered a brief smile. "Thank you." She bit her lip. "You did a great job on Mac's leg."

It was a small compliment, but Rafe wasn't used to any. His heart burned for a moment at the simple words. And as he followed Annie down the hall he stared at the happy pictures on the wall.

"How does a famous television star end up as a combat medic?"

Stepping behind the room divider, Annie tossed him his clothes. "I'll wait here. Shout when you're decent."

He hadn't meant to ask the question, but Rafe yearned to know the answer.

Quickly stripping, he pulled his jeans and T-shirt back on. "Done."

He studied the petite beauty as she stepped from the divider. Annie's bright hair was pulled into a tight bun. Her scrubs hugged her hips just enough to hint at the spectacular curves beneath them. An uncomfortable need pulled at him.

"Seriously, Annie. How did you become an Army medic?"

Annie tilted her head and shrugged. "By enlisting in the Army. Come on, I'll show you where the laundry is—since my role as hostess does not include laundry duty."

Rafe wanted more information, but Annie's shoulders were pulled tight. Swallowing his inquiries, he playfully glared at the washing machine. "Wait… Dr. Freson assured me my laundry was covered in this gig!"

"Nope—that was a lie to make the Arctic more palatable. You're on your own in cleaning your tighty-whiteys." Annie shook her head, her eyes lighting up at the joke. Her shoulders relaxed, and a bit of the tension that had clung to them since he'd called her Charlotte evaporated.

Pressing a hand against his forehead, Rafe laughed, "I haven't worn those since I was a boy, Annie. As a matter of fact, I think the last ones I owned probably had Batman or Superman on them."

Annie tossed him a packet of detergent, her eyes widened as she pulled her hands to her hips. "You liked comics?"

Tossing the scrubs into the laundry, he cut his eyes to her. "Nope—I *loved* comics. Superheroes always help people."

Crossing her arms, Annie leaned against the dryer. "Is that why you became a doctor? To help people?"

Rafe shifted under her intense scrutiny. People loved asking doctors why they'd become doctors. Most said they'd been called to help people. Annie had walked away from Hollywood, served in combat and then gone to med school. Rafe was *certain* Annie was a doctor because she wanted to help people.

Rafe wished that was his story. He could lie, or avoid the question like he usually did, but he didn't want to. "No, although that would be a better story to tell. I—I was raised in foster care."

Rafe had passed through so many houses full of kids and adults. There hadn't time for him to be given the attention he'd wanted—needed. It might have been different if he'd stayed in his first home. His foster mother Emma had cared for him. But he'd lost her too. After his mother's abandonment, Emma's passing had been too much, and he'd shut everyone out.

"I spent most of my childhood angry at the world. Got kicked out of a lot of homes for being too much to handle. I needed love and attention to deal with the loss of my parents, but there was never enough to go around. One of my foster moms idolized doctors. Said they were the best."

Rafe pulled on the back of his neck. He didn't know why he'd started this story, but the words refused to slow.

"I told her one day that I was going to be a doctor. The best doctor ever. She laughed and told me I was more likely to end up serving time than being a productive member of society—let alone a doctor."

Annie sucked in a breath and her fists clenched. "That is a horrible thing to say to anyone—but to a child…"

She was angry on his behalf? When had anyone ever been angry about what had happened to him? Rafe's swallowed the lump pushing at the back of his throat. It had always been lonely, knowing no one truly cared about him. Annie acknowledging his pain was a salve he didn't know how to handle.

Rafe stared at the ceiling. "It was cruel, but

she did me a favor. I studied every night, made it my goal to prove her wrong." Blowing out a breath, he let his gaze wander over the plain tiles. "She wasn't as impressed as I hoped when I got a scholarship."

Annie patted his arm and smiled. "Well, I think you're very impressive."

His chest heaved at the praise. She meant that—it wasn't a false platitude. Her hand disappeared from his arm and Rafe frowned. The faint scents of lavender and cleaning solution faded as she put distance between them. It had been a simple touch, but it had put a dent in the emptiness in his soul.

"Did you read a lot of comic books while you were on set?"

Gripping the edge of the dryer, Rafe clung to the cool metal to keep himself from reaching for her. Something about Annie called to a deep part of him, and he needed to remember that this was a temporary gig.

Annie's shoulders sagged and the mood in the room tilted. Wrapping her arms around herself, she seemed to shut down. "No." Her gray eyes slid to the window, a shadow of pain passing over her features before she took a deep breath.

"I learned about comics in the Army. Blake loved—" Annie closed her eyes.

Rafe hadn't meant to ask something that clearly caused her pain. He'd never served in the military, but Rafe had worked beside men and women who had. He'd seen a simple question touch a veteran in unexpected ways before. "Annie…"

She didn't look at him as she continued the story. "Blake would read them to the company as soon as his mom sent them—he made up silly voices for each of the characters. We used to laugh and joke about some of the more ridiculous plot lines, but we all loved it when those boxes arrived." Annie paused for a moment before adding, "Blake's mom still sent me boxes after—" She bit her lip before offering him a sad smile. "The good guy always wins in the comics. I wish life reflected that."

"Me too."

For a moment Rafe wondered what would happen if he put his arms around her. She needed comfort, but he barely knew her.

Before he could list all the reasons to keep his distance, Annie stepped toward the door. He knew it was the right move, but it stung.

Annie gripped the door handle. "You should

get settled. I'll check on Mac after I see to the paperwork." Without waiting for a reply, she made her escape.

Glancing at the snow flurries outside the window, Rafe swallowed. Jenn needed to get here soon. He stared at the empty space Annie had occupied; the snow was the least of his concerns.

"Any particular reason you kept my identity secret from Dr. Bradstone?" Annie pulled her wavy hair into a tight ponytail as she talked to Jenn.

"I don't think of you as Charlotte Greene."

Annie rolled her eyes; Jenn didn't think of her as Charlotte Greene, but Rafe did. She hated it that it bothered her so much.

"Rafe called me last night," said Jenn.

Of course he had…

"To talk about meeting Charlotte Greene?" It wasn't Rafe's fault the most exciting thing about her was her past.

Dishes clacked on Jenn's end. "No. He called to complain about the cold and tell me how remarkable you are."

Remarkable? Her lip twitched. She liked it that he'd called her that—too much. She knew Rafe was a wonderful doctor. And after their awkward greeting he'd been surprisingly easy to talk to.

And he was gorgeous. But she only needed his medical skills.

"Annie?" Jenn's voice was strained. "Are you still there?"

"Yep!"

That false peppy tone was her tell, and Jenn latched on. "What's wrong?"

Falling onto her mattress, Annie stared at the ceiling. "Nothing. Rafe's an excellent doctor and—"

Annie's throat seized. She didn't know the man, but she wanted to. And that was terrifying. His upbringing had been completely different than hers, but she recognized the scars of loneliness worn on his soul. She had several the same.

"He's attractive…" Jenn offered.

There was more to it as far as Annie was concerned, but those words were locked away. She was almost positive that Rafe had wanted to hug her yesterday. And, for the first time since Blake had died, she'd wanted to step into another man's arms. Wanted to feel the heat of another body, the comfort of knowing that for a moment she wasn't alone. The desire had terrified her, and she'd fled.

"He *is* gorgeous—which his legion of fans all know."

Annie strained her ears, listening for any sign that the stunning doctor was awake.

"There isn't anything else to talk about, Jenn." Ignoring Jenn's sigh, Annie pressed on. "I enjoyed talking to him yesterday, but he's only here a few weeks."

"Perfect for a fling, then."

Annie felt her chin hit her chest at Jenn's suggestion. "A *fling*?"

Jenn's laughter was contagious, and Annie placed a hand over her mouth to quiet her giggles.

"Why not? He's hot—you're hot." She giggled again before sobering. "I worry about you. You've been alone since…"

Jenn's pause tore through Annie's happy bubble. "Since Blake was killed."

Her former fiancé's name danced around the room. She never talked about Blake—except she'd talked about Blake's love of comics with Rafe yesterday. Rafe's eyes had lit up when she'd mentioned comics—just like Blake's had.

"Annie…"

"I need to see a patient."

"Give Rafe a chance, Annie. I bet he's very skilled with his hands!"

Annie glared at her phone before looking out the window. Rafe was standing outside without a coat—*again.*

She stood up. "I'm getting off the phone now, Dr. Freson."

Jenn was still chuckling as Annie disconnected.

Pulling on her coat, Annie ran through the clinic. Flinging open the front door, she almost fell into Rafe's arms. Despite his chilly embrace, her body sang.

Annie pulled him inside. "What are you *doing*?" She made herself step back, hating the bloom of fire flicking across her skin.

Rafe shivered and blew into his hands before pushing a few buttons on his phone. "Trying to get a good picture of the mountains to load onto my social media. They are beautiful."

Social media?

Annie rolled her eyes. She'd been worried about him—raced like a madwoman to rescue him. But Rafe was risking frostbite to impress people he didn't know. It was ridiculous.

Annie wanted to shake him. Grabbing his cold

fingers, she clasped them between her palms. "These are nearly frozen!"

She knew Rafe was capable of warming his own appendages, but she couldn't force herself to let go. He was too attractive, too smooth— too much for her. Annie wanted to yell at him for being foolish, and she also wanted to close the tiny distance between them.

That was dangerous. Getting close to the temporary Dr. Rafe Bradstone wasn't an option.

Rafe swallowed as Annie's soft hands viciously rubbed his aching fingers. He hadn't expected to be outside for so long, or for the cold to seep into his bones so quickly. Needles shot through his fingers as blood returned to the frozen digits. The sensation was uncomfortable, and it kept him from feeling Annie's touch.

He'd lain awake last night, thinking of her, replaying the conversation, wishing he'd hugged her. It was silly. He barely knew her. But that missed opportunity refused to leave his mind.

"I can feel them again." Rafe regretted the words instantly when Annie dropped his hands.

"This isn't the set for a television show, Rafe." Annie's cheeks were tinged with heat as she glared at him.

Television show? This had nothing to do with his role on *Dr. Dave.* He was so much more than a television doctor. Rafe wanted her to understand that—needed her to see him as more than a pretty face on a talk show.

His phone dinged as fans started interacting with his post, destroying his planned denial. "I know that, Annie." Rafe shook his head as he stepped closer.

"*Do* you?" Annie glared at his pocket, where his phone continued to buzz. "Then put on a coat and a good pair of boots if you insist on posting Arctic pictures. Unless you're trying to demonstrate what frostbite looks like?" She turned on her heel.

He should let her go, but he didn't want to start the day off on the wrong foot. "Annie?" Rafe moved quickly, halting her retreat.

She raised an eyebrow as his phone buzzed with more notifications. Those pings usually brought him a bit of joy. Knowing that others enjoyed his thoughts and pictures made him feel wanted—briefly. Under Annie's gaze it felt shallow. He shifted as the uncomfortable feeling rolled through him.

Reaching in his pocket, Rafe silenced his

phone. "Thank you for checking on me. I will not venture outside again without a coat. Promise."

Annie nodded before offering a small smile. The upturn of her full lips sent a thrill racing down his spine. She was perfection—and not for him. This was a temporary assignment, and this morning had certainly proved that he didn't belong in the Arctic.

Except that for a moment, when she'd been in his arms, he'd wanted to. That terrified him.

Annie's skin tingled as she raced for the back of the clinic. She'd only meant to warm up his fingers for a minute, but if Rafe hadn't told her that he could feel his fingers again she'd have kept holding him.

She was just lonely. Lust wasn't love.

Her heart clenched as she leaned against the door to her office. *Love.* She'd had a chance at love, and it had been terribly short-lived.

The few dates she'd been on in the last several years had been unqualified disasters. The men she met were only interested in her past. After the last catastrophe had resulted in her date attempting to sell photos of them to a tabloid, Annie had retreated from the dating pool. Romance had never crossed her mind.

Until Rafe.

Her heart pounded as his name reverberated around his brain. It was nothing. She'd been worried about a colleague—that was why she'd rushed to his side this morning.

And yesterday?

Swallowing, Annie tried to rationalize her need to talk to Rafe then. It had seemed natural, because Rafe's love of comics had reminded her of the man she'd lost. That was all...

Blake.

Annie never discussed her fiancé. Even Jenn knew not to ask about the lanky man who'd played such an important role in getting her to Alaska.

Blake had been the only person in her boot camp to see past Annie's Hollywood image. The Army, even with its demanding routines and shouting sergeants, had been her first taste of freedom. Making friends hadn't been easy— everyone had seen her as soft or, worse, thought she'd joined to get publicity—but Blake had given Annie the idea of adding an additional thirty pounds to her rucksack for the company's ten-mile run. That stunt hadn't earned her many new friends, but the whispers had turned into a quiet respect.

She and Blake had become as inseparable as the Army would allow. She'd cried when he'd been assigned to the Cavalry, rather than medic training with her. And most of their relationship had occurred in the brief R & R weeks they'd carved out.

Blake had proposed in Germany, on the night before he'd headed back to Iraq. She'd worn his ring for less than a week before being called into her commander's office…

The smell of mint aftershave interrupted her thoughts as Rafe leaned over her shoulder to grab a patient's file.

"You okay?" Tilting his head, he narrowed his eyes as they focused on her posture.

"Fine."

Rafe's eyes widened at Annie's clipped response, but he didn't push. Leaning against the wall he wiggled his fingers. "I really am sorry I gave you a scare this morning."

"Sorry I scolded you. They're your fingers and toes." Annie laughed.

How did Rafe manage to put her at ease and make her so uncomfortable all at once?

"Mac's wife just got here. I told her he could go home and come back at the end of next week so we can remove the stitches. He made a cheeky comment about his plans for when he gets home."

Her fingers brushed his as he passed her the clipboard with Mac's recent vitals. Her heart jumped as she forced her eyes not to linger in the chocolate depths of his.

"Mac's going to be a real terror. Luckily Molly is up to the task of keeping him in line."

Rafe let out a low laugh. "They sound like they're something."

"Been in love for more than half their lives." Annie knew her wistful tone carried down the hall before she pushed away from the wall.

"Dr. Masters is a romantic?" Rafe tapped her shoulder with the chart as he followed her into the office.

"You think so?" She had been—once. Annie tapped a pen against the chart as she studied Rafe. "Are you?"

Rafe looked up from Mac's chart, crinkles darting at the corner of his eyes. "Am I what?"

"Are you a romantic?" Annie swallowed, and her gray eyes refused to meet his.

"No. Love doesn't last, so why bother with romance?"

"That is a sad statement."

* * *

Rafe's chest felt tight as Annie frowned. He should have made a pithy comment about roses and boxes of chocolates. That would have been the safe conversation topic—not his actual thoughts on whatever people meant when they said love.

For some reason Rafe seemed incapable of keeping his distance from Annie. That was dangerous. Rafe was leaving, and she didn't approve of "television doctors."

When Annie had fallen into his arms that morning, he'd wanted to hold her. Had wanted to kiss away the tiny line that appeared between her eyebrows when she frowned. His mind spun. Annie was smart, talented and gorgeous, but that didn't have to mean anything. Even if they had chemistry, it would only result in disaster.

"The emotion we call 'love' is just the brain releasing norepinephrine and dopamine. The scientific studies on brain chemistry are fascinating, but most people don't spend their free time reading scientific journals." Rafe shrugged.

Annie's fingers twitched and an emotion he couldn't read spread across her face. "No. What you're describing is lust and attraction. Love is so much more."

The certainty in her voice shot through him. What made her so certain?

"Then what is love?" Rafe leaned against her desk, his eyes hovering over her. This wasn't a conversation they should be having so early in the morning—or at all—but he was intrigued. What made Annie so sure about love that her eyes glistened?

"Love is *life*. Smiling, fighting, tension, joy…" Annie pursed her lips. "And pain."

Rafe understood pain, but before he could agree Annie continued.

"It's the promise that you're never really alone. The realization that even when you're so angry with each other, life would be empty without your partner. It's knowing that if you're separated by oceans, there's still someone who is on your side. A person who will fight *for* you and *with* you. Someone who will always choose you. It's everything."

Annie had evidently loved someone deeply—Blake?—and yet she was alone. Rafe clenched his fists. She'd given so much of herself to someone and they'd left her. He was a little jealous that she could argue that love existed after the man she'd cared for had clearly chosen some other life.

Rafe's heart pounded in his chest. He wanted her definition to be true. "That is a beautiful sentiment."

"But you don't believe it?" Annie's eyes searched his, but he didn't know what she was looking for.

"I want it to be true…" Rafe's words faded. He wanted to believe someone could choose him over everything else. But if even his mother hadn't chosen him, why would anyone else?

Rafe smiled as his insides twisted. "We are having a very deep conversation before 10:00 a.m., Dr. Masters."

A soft chuckle left her lips and Annie pulled at the stack of patient files in front of her. "We have a full schedule today. I think most of the women in town are hoping you'll give them a well-check."

"Annie—"

The front doorbell chimed and Annie headed for the door without looking back. "I'll take Mrs. Anderson. You get Mrs. Hillard."

Glancing at his phone, Rafe stared at the reaction to his snow post. He waited for the bubble of happiness it usually brought, but the rising count of "likes" felt fake. Rafe glared at his phone for a moment before shutting it off.

* * *

"Your blood pressure is elevated, Mrs. Hillard."

"Really?" Touching his arm, Mrs. Hillard leaned in close. "So, what are you doing to help with the Fall Carnival?"

He pulled away and stared at the grin on his patient's face. They needed to focus on her blood pressure not some carnival.

Offering a pat on her wrinkled hand, Rafe tried his "firm but friendly" tone. "Is there a history of high blood pressure in your family?"

Green eyes sparkled at him through thick glasses. "Don't know. Now, the carnival—what would you like to do?"

"Do…?" Rubbing his face, Rafe reached for some patience. Leaning against his desk, Rafe smiled at his elderly patient. "I don't know anything about the carnival, but I'm happy to discuss it after we talk about your blood pressure. Elevated blood pressure puts you at an increased risk for heart attack, heart failure, organ failure and stroke. It's serious."

Mrs. Hillard smiled at him. "I'm not worried about those things."

Crossing his arms, Rafe tried to keep the frustration out of his voice. "Mrs. Hillard. This is serious."

"I'll be eighty next summer."

"And you're exceptionally healthy otherwise." Rafe sighed, wondering how to make her understand.

Mrs. Hillard's eyes shimmered for a moment. "My Thomas has been gone for two years, Dr. Bradstone. He was my everything. Now I'm just kicking it—as my great-grandson says—until I meet my maker."

Rafe didn't have any words to follow that declaration. He couldn't tell her he understood.

Pursing his lips, he tried another tack. "What is the Fall Carnival?"

Mrs. Hillard's tongue pushed against the small gap between her front teeth as she smiled. "The whole community takes part. There are games, food—and the dance competition."

"Dance competition?"

"It started a few years ago." Her finger tapped her chin before she shrugged. "I don't remember why, but people perform routines in costume. The winner gets a silly trophy. It's great fun, and all the money raised goes to the library. It's my favorite time of year."

This was clearly important to her. Rafe raised an eyebrow and took a shot. "If I agree to do anything you want at the carnival, will you follow a diet and exercise plan for a few weeks? If that doesn't lower your blood pressure, will you consider taking medication? I'm sure your husband doesn't want you joining him before a few more Fall Carnivals."

Mrs. Hillard studied him. "I might be willing to make that deal. Do you dance?"

"Only a little."

That wasn't exactly true, but Rafe didn't feel like explaining. His agent Carrie had insisted he take lessons. She'd claimed it would help him land a role on a reality dancing competition. And he was a natural, according to his dance instructor—just like his father.

That was the comparison he'd feared—and hated. Before his death, Rafe's mother had always cooed about how much he looked like his father. He was an exact replica. But it was that resemblance that had turned her love into neglect and finally to hatred. If he looked like his father, danced like his father, how long into a relationship before he managed to destroy any woman who cared for him?

"Fantastic. Another couple dancing will bring in more money. Your job is to be Dr. A's partner for the dance." Mrs. Hillard clapped her hands and her eyes darted to the door.

"Dance with Annie?"

Rafe's tongue felt dry even as Mrs. Hillard's eyes glittered. He wanted to pull Annie into his arms, spin her around the floor and explore the heat that struck him each time their hands brushed. Wanted it too much...

"What if I make the cotton candy?"

"I have the Jones boys making cotton candy." Mrs. Hillard reached for her coat. "It's for charity. The other groups have been dancing together for years—the families really get into it."

"I'll talk to Dr. Masters."

Rafe was surprised as those words tumbled forward. He'd meant to say no—explain that he might not even be in town. What if he asked Annie and she said no? What if she said yes?

"I'll mark you down. Just remind Dr. A that the library needs a new children's section." Mrs. Hillard grabbed the notes Rafe had made about diet and exercise as she headed for the door. "Nice to meet you, Dr. Bradstone."

"Schedule your follow-up for six weeks from today!" Rafe called as the spry woman raced down the hall. "And follow the instructions on those papers!"

"A deal is a deal!" Mrs. Hillard laughed as she disappeared.

Annie's chuckle hit his back.

Spinning, he crossed his arms. "Was that a test, Dr. A?"

Annie pulled her chin to her chest. Her eyes sparkled. "No…"

"You're covering your mouth, hoping I won't notice the smirk! You *did* give me a difficult patient."

Lowering her hand, Annie shrugged. "It wasn't a test—not really. I've been attempting to get Nancy Hillard to take her blood pressure seriously for the last year. Guess I was hoping your charms would work."

"You think I have charms?"

Rafe had meant it as a joke, but he studied Annie as she stared at him. He wanted her to say yes; he wanted her to be intrigued by him too. That was a ridiculous desire, but he couldn't quiet it.

Pursing her lips, Annie held his gaze. "I think you know you're charming. Did my plan work?"

Cocking his head, Rafe smiled. "I made her a deal. She's promised to try a diet and exercise program and consider medication if it doesn't work."

"Wonderful!"

Annie's smile warmed his insides. Rafe wanted

to bask in it, but he took a deep breath. "And in return we're partners for the Fall Carnival dance. She drives a hard bargain."

Annie's eyes widened, and her tongue darted around her lips as she stared at him. "I can't be your partner for the Monster Mash."

Rafe refused to acknowledge the pain that statement caused. It didn't matter that she didn't want to dance with him—it *didn't*.

He raised an eyebrow. "Monster Mash?"

"What else would you call a charity dance during Halloween? The whole town cheers the contestants. It's a lovely spectacle."

He watched as Annie crossed her arms. She was being oddly defensive of a dance she didn't want to participate in.

"She said to remind you the library needs a new children's section." Leaning closer, Rafe tried to ignore Annie's soft scent. "Don't make me use my charms."

Annie opened her mouth and then closed it. She offered him a tight smile. "Sorry, Rafe. I can't dance with you."

"It's for a good cause," Rafe pressed.

He knew he should drop it, but he wanted her to say yes.

Choose me...

"I guess it *is* for a good cause..." Annie looked at him, her teeth dug deep into her lip.

"If you keep biting like that, it's going to start bleeding."

Rafe ran his thumb over her lip, pulling it from her teeth before dropping his hand. His ears burned as he stared at her. His tongue stuck to the roof of his mouth as he tried to determine if he should apologize or make a flirty statement. Neither action felt right.

Annie's fingers brushed over her lips before she offered him a soft smile. "The library does need a new children's section."

Her hip swept against his as she slid her chart into the file holder behind him.

"I haven't danced in years, but it's nice you want to participate. Let Mrs. Hillard know that I'm too stubborn. She won't have any issue finding another partner for you. I bet several of your fans would love to spend the evening dancing with Dr. Bradstone. She could even auction it off, raise more—"

"I don't want to be auctioned off!"

Rafe hadn't meant to interrupt. Hadn't meant to be so defensive, but he didn't want a fan. He wanted Annie. Heat pulsed through him as the scent of lavender touched him. Swallowing, he slid Mrs. Hillard's file into place and picked up the next patient's—anything to keep his fingers from reaching for Annie again.

"Sorry, Rafe."

Stepping away from her, Rafe raised his chin. It was a silly Fall Carnival dance; he'd been turned down for so many other things it didn't matter.

Nodding, Rafe shrugged as he looked over the next patient's file. "I'll probably be back in LA by then anyway. It was a dumb idea."

Annie's lips slid open, but Rafe didn't stay to hear her excuse. His Alaskan residency had a termination date; he just needed to find a way to put distance between him and Annie until then. It would be easier if they weren't working and living together—easier if he actually wanted to put distance between them—but he was not going to make a fool of himself with another starlet—not even Annie.

CHAPTER THREE

AN ALARM RACED through Rafe's dreams. Rubbing his eyes, he tried to orient himself. Where was that pinging noise coming from?

Stepping into the hallway, Rafe followed the noise to Annie's room. A flashing red light caught his eye. The pinging was coming from an alarm next to her empty bed. What was going on?

"Annie?"

Rafe started toward the kitchen. The door leading down to the clinic stood wide open. *An emergency.* Rafe's heart pounded as he raced down the stairs.

"He jumped from the bed." A frantic sob echoed from the first examination room. "I put the boys in bunk beds when they moved into my apartment. I didn't think—"

"Deep breaths, Maggie. It's a small fracture on the ulna."

Annie's calm voice floated toward Rafe as he

stepped into the room. An X-ray of a tiny arm hung on the wall. Clearly he'd missed most of the action.

Why hadn't she woken him? Their professional relationship was excellent. He might have retreated from all personal interaction over the last two days, but this was why he was here—to help.

She'd asked him to dinner last night and he'd made an excuse about needing to work. When he'd drifted into the kitchen an hour later Annie had been gone. It was probably for the best. Since Annie had declined the dancing invitation there had been no more deep conversations about comics or love.

He missed them.

"Jonah just needs a cast," said Annie.

The young woman, Maggie, barely glanced at Rafe as he stepped up next to Annie. A boy who couldn't be more than five lay whimpering on the table.

"I want the top bunk."

"It's mine." A sullen boy who might be around eight yawned from the corner. "Could have just left me at home, Maggie."

"You're seven, Chris. I'm not leaving you home alone."

"Mom always did."

"Not now, Chris." Maggie sighed.

"You're not Dr. Henkle." Jonah's voice was weak with exhaustion and pain as he stared at Rafe.

"Nope. I'm Dr. Bradstone, and I'm going to help Dr. A get you feeling better."

Jonah's eyes shifted between him, and Annie.

"Now comes the important question." Annie winked at Jonah. "What color cast do you want, little man?"

His eyes widened, but he didn't hesitate. "Blue."

Annie yawned as she reached for the stockinette and padding. She was clearly exhausted.

"Why don't I do the cast?" said Rafe.

Shocks traveled up his arms as his fingers brushed hers. He held her eyes for a moment before focusing on Jonah's gaze.

"I had a blue cast when I was about your brother's age. I got it falling off a friend's bike."

Jonah didn't say anything, but Annie mouthed *thank you* as she leaned against the wall. She and Maggie made small talk while Rafe plastered Jonah's arm. When it was finally set, Annie carried Jonah to Maggie's car while Rafe grabbed his sleeping brother.

"Sorry it's so late, Dr. A." Maggie sighed as

she buckled Jonah in. "I keep second-guessing myself. Everything seems so hard…" Maggie ruffled Chris' hair before opening her car door.

"You're doing great." Annie offered her a quick hug, then waved the small trio off before trudging back to the clinic.

Annie yawned as she locked the door. "Sorry— I forgot to turn the alarm off when I hit the bottom of the steps."

"It's fine, Annie." Rafe smiled and yawned too but made no move to head back to his room. "I'm here to help. You should have gotten me."

Despite her exhaustion, Annie had no desire to go back to bed. Rafe hadn't immediately retreated. If the wall he'd placed between them was down, Annie didn't want to rush away.

He'd barely said two words to her since she'd declined his dance offer. She'd expected him to jump at the opportunity to auction off his time at the dance, to bask in the worship of the television doctor, but she'd misread him. She'd spent her whole childhood being misread by fans and critics. She'd hurt Rafe with her assumptions, and she hated the distance he'd put between them.

She missed their easy conversations, the few fun moments they'd shared. She wanted to fix it, but Rafe no longer seemed interested in dinner conversation or breakfast banter. And she wanted to dance with him. That worried her—but not finding a way to bridge the gap between them worried her more.

The stubble along Rafe's strong jaw gave him a rugged look. How did anyone look at him and not imagine kissing him? Annie rubbed her eyes. She was exhausted and letting her brain wander to places it shouldn't.

"Do you answer many 2:00 a.m. calls?"

Rafe's eyes were hooded, but there was a spark of concern behind them. Or maybe she just wanted there to be.

"Some. The nearest hospital is almost three hours away. If it's something I can fix…"

"Where's their mom? Maggie barely seems old enough to care for two young boys." Rafe's voice was tight, and his eyes stared past her.

Annie nodded. "Their mother has substance abuse issues and is serving time. Maggie is twenty and just got custody of her brothers."

Rafe let out a low whistle. "Lucky boys. The system isn't any place to grow up." Rafe shuddered, and Annie put her hand on his. Rafe stared at it for a moment but didn't pull away.

"They are lucky, but Maggie still fears she'll turn out like her mom."

Rafe shook his head. "I understand. I can't imagine wanting to pass on *my* family genetics to the next generation. My parents' genes were all bad."

"No, they weren't!"

How could he think that? He'd spent the last hour being kind to a tired, hurt child while casting his arm. He'd answered every one of Jonah's questions. He'd been the perfect doctor. And her heart had sung as she'd watched him.

Rafe raised an eyebrow. "You didn't know them."

"But I know *you*."

Or I want to.

Annie's breath caught as Rafe's chocolate eyes held hers. It was too late for this conversation, but she saw the hurt bubbling under the surface. He didn't see himself clearly, and he should. Rafe was amazing.

"Their genes are in you, and you turned into an intelligent, caring man. You literally help people for a living, Rafe."

Annie bounced on her feet as he stared at her. He was so close, but still he didn't say anything.

"My mother wasn't great at the parenting thing

either—doesn't mean I don't want kids some-day," she said.

Annie wanted to push those words back in. Exhaustion was loosening her tongue—or maybe it was just Rafe's effect on her.

Swallowing, she pointed to the clock. Maybe tomorrow she'd find a way to broach the topic of the dance. "We should try to catch a few hours of sleep."

Annie's heart pounded. She liked being close to him. But she was too tired to try to work out those feelings.

"Who is Dr. Henkle? Is he related to the pilot and his wife who flew me out?"

Rafe hadn't meant to ask any questions, but despite the late hour he wasn't ready to say good-night.

"Dr. Henkle is their son and my business partner." Annie paused outside her door.

Her eyes shone, but the dark circles under them worried him. She was so used to doing everything on her own she hadn't even thought to get him tonight. This "partner" couldn't be much help.

"Partner?" Rafe's mind twisted around the word. Was this the man Annie had thought of when she was explaining love? "Where is he, then?"

A shadow crossed over Annie's eyes before she shrugged. "Liam travels a lot. He serves the remote communities."

"But Blue Ash is a remote community." Surely her partner should be alleviating some of her burden?

"No, it isn't. Not exactly anyway. The roads here can be used for most of the winter. Planes can reach us… There are villages farther north that only see a doctor when Liam arrives."

"Why not hire another physician?"

Annie didn't answer, but her fists clenched.

It was too late to argue, but Rafe couldn't stop the flow of words. Annie must handle after-hours calls far more frequently than she wanted to admit—Rafe was almost sure of it.

"If it's a monetary issue, you could probably use your fame—"

"Are you *kidding* me?"

"No, I just— I only…"

The words died on his lips as fire shot from her gray eyes. She was lonely and tired, even if she wouldn't admit it.

Her eyes still glittered as she stepped toward him. "Why do you think Jenn is coming? Liam and I have hired two doctors over the last three years. Neither was willing to stay past October. As you've pointed out, we're remote by most people's standards."

"I'm sorry." He flinched as she turned her face away from him. "I worry about you." The words were out and he couldn't take them back—didn't want to. "You deserve a break. Who helps you?"

"A break?" Annie's features softened. "Like dancing at the carnival?"

All the oxygen seemed to have evaporated from the small hallway. How had she flipped this conversation? It didn't matter.

Rafe leaned against the door and smiled. "I was thinking more of a vacation, but dancing is good for stress relief."

Annie's cheeks flamed as she met his gaze and looked away. "I heard there was a physician who needed a partner."

"It *is* for a good cause." Rafe smiled.

"True." Annie laughed. "I'm sorry I misread your offer. I figured you'd prefer a fan to a washed-up actress."

"You aren't a washed-up actress, Annie." Rafe pushed a tight curl behind her ear. "You're an intelligent, caring woman."

He winked as he repeated the compliment she'd

given him. He wanted to kiss her, to close the tiny distance between them, but he was afraid she'd back away if he moved.

Annie smiled. "If you don't mind a rusty dancer I would like to be your partner—*dance* partner."

Rafe's breath hitched as she offered him a quick hug. Her curls trailed along his chin, but the contact was too short.

"I promise not to step on your toes. Thanks for your help tonight. It's nice not to do everything alone."

Then she was gone.

Rafe was just drifting back to sleep when he realized Annie had avoided his question.

No one helped Annie.

Rafe's heart twisted. She was alone, and she needed more than a temporary doctor could provide. He'd make certain that she understood he was available for all after-hours calls. At least that way he'd relieve a bit of her burden for a few weeks—and he was looking forward to her stepping on his toes...

Rafe slammed the screen on his laptop and winced as the noise reverberated around the kitchen. Carrie had sent three emails today. She'd tried to schedule two video interviews for him and she wasn't taking his refusal well. It didn't help that she'd seen he'd lost a few dozen subscribers on his social media profile. He'd been gaining followers for the last several months— he wasn't now.

Rafe's stomach tossed at his agent's pointed questions regarding his lack of new social media posts. He usually posted a few times a day, but after Annie had chastised him for chasing followers in the cold he hadn't posted again. He'd started several, but hadn't published any.

In the week he'd spent with Annie time had flown. His social media profile hadn't seemed important. His need for "likes" faded when Annie was near. He'd taken to counting the number of times he made her laugh or smile instead. The joy those moments brought lasted longer than the pings on his phone.

He wasn't going to be around Annie forever, though. He had a life in LA, and a career—a plan to make his place on *Dr. Dave* permanent. Carrie's reminder now that Dave was monitoring his social media accounts stung.

"Everything okay?" Annie's fingers brushed his as she passed him a cookie.

"Sure." It wasn't really a lie, but his stomach flipped as Annie raised her eyebrow.

Rafe bit into the cookie, making sure to keep his eyes focused on the plate. Since her late-night declaration about him being an amazing man, he'd had a hard time meeting her gaze. He wanted it to be true—wanted to be worthy of someone as magnificent as Annie.

The cookie stuck against his throat as he thought about Carrie's emails. He still hadn't told Annie about his agent being her mom. He wasn't hiding it—not really.

Nibbling on her own cookie, Annie interrupted his tense thoughts. "My friend Holly makes the best baked goods. For two years, she made cookies and cakes out of her small kitchen. A few weeks ago, she opened a bakery in town. I still haven't managed to sneak over there, but Holly delivers!"

Annie handed him another, and gold shimmered in her eyes as she laid her hand over his. "What's wrong?"

Her nails were painted a light pink, but the skin around her thumb was still red and raw. What had she done?

Rafe rubbed his finger along her palm, before

forcing himself to pull away. He wanted to touch her more than he'd ever wanted to touch another woman. He had assumed the need would pass, but it had only grown.

Since fixing Jonah's arm they'd worked together every day, before retiring to Annie's apartment. When they'd done the dishes last night, Annie's hip had bumped his several times. Rafe had studied his ceiling well past midnight as he'd weighed up whether she was interested in touching him too.

Annie leaned over the table and tapped his nose, "Earth to Rafe?"

Laughing, he squinted at her. "Sorry, I was just plotting how to get you onto a dance floor."

He'd tried to schedule their first practice a few times, but she'd always managed to duck the appointment. He wanted to dance with her, hold her in his arms—maybe then his need to touch her would disappear.

Annie's blush spread across her cheeks and neck. "We don't need much practice—no changing the subject. What's wrong?"

"Nothing." Rafe bit his tongue as he rushed the word out. Pain ripped across his mouth. "Hell!"

Annie chuckled as she leaned back in her chair. "See—there are consequences for lying."

Rafe stuck out his injured tongue. "Fine— you're right."

"I know I am. What's going on? I'm a pretty good listener."

"My agent's getting a lot of requests for me to do interviews. She's angry I'm not responding." *His agent*—he'd failed to use Carrie's name again.

Annie's brows knitted together as she picked at her thumb. "You're avoiding your agent?"

Avoiding. That descriptor didn't seem quite right, but as he sat with Annie the tiny pull he'd felt to answer Carrie disappeared. LA seemed so insignificant when he was sitting in Annie's homey kitchen.

He frowned as Annie whittled at the skin by her nail, then reached for her hand. Desire flooded him as her fingers wrapped around his. "You're going to make yourself bleed," he said.

"Probably." She frowned at the broken skin. "Sorry—it's my nervous habit."

"Do I make you nervous?"

She made *him* nervous. More with each passing day. Annie Masters made him think about topics he wanted to bury. His parents, his character, his desire to know what she tasted like, if her body would flush with pleasure…

"Yes."

Before Rafe could process that answer, Annie rushed on.

"Are you going to do the interviews?"

"No." It was an easy answer.

Squeezing his hand, Annie lifted her chin. "Why?"

"Because I'm here."

The interviews would help his chances at landing a permanent spot on *Dr. Dave*, but what if people realized he was here with Annie? Dave would chase *that* story. Rafe wasn't willing to share his precious time with her. Besides, she'd worked hard to get away from Hollywood. He was not going to bring it to her doorstep.

Annie squeezed his hand again before she pulled away. "Are you hiding here?"

Looking at his hand, Rafe frowned. He wanted to reach for her again. Panic shot through him as her eyes held his.

"Why would I hide?" he asked.

She raised both her eyebrows. "Vanessa Hutchinson?"

"I didn't realize you read the gossip magazines."

Rafe tapped his fingers against the table, hating the defensive tone in his voice. Was that why she'd initially said no to dancing with him?

"The clinic has a subscription to a few. And I…" Annie's voice faded as she looked at him. "I *may* have read a few articles before you arrived." She bit her lip as her eyes floated over his. "I'm sorry, Rafe. I know they're trash. I know that you didn't cheat on Vanessa."

"How do you know?"

Rafe leaned forward. Dave and a few of his colleagues had all snickered about how he'd messed up a perfect thing. People who should have known his character had believed him capable of hurting someone he cared about.

"I guess…"

Why did she know it?

Annie stared at Rafe. He wasn't a cheater; she didn't know why she was so certain, but she was.

"I think you're too good of a person to do something so dishonorable. Am I right?" Annie held her breath.

"I didn't cheat on her." Rafe let out a breath and a bit of tension leaked from his shoulders.

"Vanessa isn't interested in correcting the press and I don't want to answer questions."

"I'm sorry she didn't correct the story. Hollywood's lights can be blinding."

Rafe laughed. "At least you don't have to worry about their glare here. This is the perfect place to get away from it all."

Annie's belly twisted. Rafe was right—this was the perfect place to hide from the nagging cameras and questions. But that wasn't what she was doing.

It wasn't.

She took another bite of cookie, focusing on the explosion of orange and sugar until it almost drove the niggle of worry from her mind.

Eventually Annie stood and dumped the last of the cold tea down the sink. When she turned Rafe was behind her. Heat poured from his chest as he held her gaze.

"Thank you for seeing the best in me."

Rafe's soft words brushed against her skin, and Annie wrapped her hands around his waist without thinking. His muscular arms captured hers and she stared at him. His lips were so close…

Rafe made her feel things she'd thought lost when she'd buried Blake. When he talked to her he was interested in her present more than her past. When she was around him the specter of Charlotte Greene disappeared.

If she didn't move now she would kiss him.

He let her go, and Annie's soul cried as she put some distance between them. *Coward.* Her brain screamed for her to run back into his arms, but the moment was gone.

"Want to help me at the community center tonight?" Annie placed a hand over her hot cheek.

"Of course. Are we going to practice our dancing?"

"Nope!" Annie smiled. If she stepped into his arms again it would be impossible to ignore the connection between them. What if she risked it and lost everything? "We'll be painting—so change into something you don't mind getting dirty."

"All right." Rafe paused before he left the kitchen. "Annie…?"

She raised an eyebrow. "I promise it's really not too messy. Are you having second thoughts about joining me?"

"Never."

Her heart leapt at the admission even as he

leaned against the door. His coffee-colored eyes held hers.

"We're going to dance tonight too."

"Is the snow bad tonight?" Rafe ran his hands along his knees as he stared out the window.

"No." Annie frowned.

A light dusting of snow covered the road, but the lazy flakes floating down were hardly worth mentioning.

"Then why are your knuckles turning white?"

The car slid slightly as Annie released her death grip.

"Sorry!"

Her cry echoed in the truck's cab as Rafe's hands flew to the dashboard.

A chill shot down Annie's back and she reached to turn the heat up. Rafe's fingers brushed hers and electricity shot up her arm. The memory of their hug burned through her. If life had a rewind button Annie would replay that scene. Kiss Rafe and hope it would be enough.

It wouldn't be...

Rafe's phone buzzed and he laughed as he checked the message. "I know social media is a necessity these days, but a fan has just asked me to help chaperone their kid's dance. Does anyone expect someone they don't know to say yes to that?"

Annie shook her head, but what was she supposed to say? She didn't think social media *was* necessary. It was a good reminder that Rafe belonged to a different world. She'd tasted that Hollywood dream and its bitterness still stung her.

Leaning her head against the seat-back, Annie forced her fingers to hold the wheel normally. The emotions raging through her warred with her need for self-protection. It should be easy to stay away from Rafe. Except everything about the man besides his connection to Tinseltown called to her.

She relaxed around Rafe, laughed with him, was just Annie with him. Rafe fit into the clinic and into her life perfectly. It was wonderful and terrifying. Attraction, longing, need—those were things Annie had set aside.

Until Rafe…

Parking the truck, Annie shifted in her seat.

She froze as Rafe's eyes held hers.

Rafe's finger pushed a stray curl behind her ear, scorching her cheek. Annie stared at his lips. He was going to kiss her. *Finally!* Would he kiss with wild abandon or soft, delicate brushes?

"Annie…?" Rafe leaned back, zipped his coat

and wrapped his scarf around his neck. "Are we waiting for someone?"

Her tongue refused to move. She'd completely misread his intentions. Had she misread the situation in the kitchen? Maybe she was just lonely and looking for a connection that wasn't there. Her lip trembled, and she hated the hurt blooming in her belly.

Pulling on the reserves she'd developed on set as a child, Annie straightened her shoulders. She would pretend everything was fine. Besides—it was. Tonight was about painting and dancing—nothing more.

"Nope. It's just us tonight." The bright tone was the standard voice she'd used as Charlotte Greene. It wasn't real, but it put people at ease.

"You sound weird…" Rafe's eyes wandered across her face.

Sucking in a breath, Annie opened the truck's door. "I'm fine. You won't need the scarf."

"You were very serious about my need for correct winter attire. I'm not going to disappoint you again." Rafe chuckled—but it wasn't his deep, cheerful laugh.

Did he know she'd wanted a kiss? Was he embarrassed for her?

It didn't matter—mustn't matter.

Annie marched to the community center door, grateful she could blame her warm cheeks on the frozen wind.

Annie was staying a few paces ahead of him, her step quickening whenever he got beside her.

He'd thought she'd kiss him earlier, but she'd just offered a hug. It wasn't enough. Then he'd hesitated a moment too long in the car, and now that moment was gone too.

That bright, cheerful voice was Annie's "Charlotte tone." He'd labeled it that after watching her deal with a patient who'd wanted to discuss the finer points of the show's final season with her. She slipped into it whenever she was putting distance between herself and others. It had been directed at him when they'd first met, but he hadn't realized what it meant. Now—it stung.

Pictures covered the entrance hall. The residents of Blue Ash captured with deep smiles as they watched plays, ate barbecue and danced at the community center. The changing fashions marked years of fun.

An image of Annie dressed in a knee-length black dress, green stockings and a pointed hat caught his attention. "You make a very cute witch."

Laughing, Annie began pulling the covers off ghosts, witches and candy corn. "Thank you. I've used that costume for all four Fall Carnivals I've been to. I heard a rumor that there's a bet on when I'll finally retire it."

Rafe studied the happy families. He knew several of the people in these pictures already. "Think they'll put up one of us when we win the dance competition?"

It would be nice knowing that part of him remained in Blue Ash after he went back to LA.

"About the dance competition—" Annie started.

"Nope." Rafe interrupted. "We are practicing tonight. You and I are going to hold that silly stuffed bear trophy high and have our picture taken."

Blue Ash was incredible. Each and every one of his patients had invited him to the Fall Carnival. Life here was slower than LA, but the hours skipped by with a comfortableness he didn't remember feeling before. If it wasn't for his place on *Dr. Dave* this town could feel like home.

Home...

The word echoed in his brain and he froze. That word had never held much meaning for

Rafe. It was just a word for a thing he'd never seemed to have and didn't need. Except now, standing next to Annie, staring at a wall full of fun, Rafe had a hard time convincing himself he didn't want it.

Annie's hip bumped his as she handed him a brush. "Do you want the ghost or the witch?"

He pursed his lips. "The ghost?"

Annie grinned at him before passing a large can of white paint. "And after you splash all that white on you get to tackle the candy cutouts."

"That was a trap!" Looking over his shoulder, Rafe shuddered playfully at the stacks of colored cutouts in desperate need of a fresh coat of paint. All contained at least three different colors and multiple patterns. "Maybe I'll take the witch…"

Hugging her paint can, Annie picked up the witch. "Oh, no. First choice is final!"

Laughing, he popped the top off the white paint. "I could argue you were deceitful, Doctor."

"Prove it, Doctor!" She winked.

His phone dinged and Rafe set it to silent.

"More DMs?" Annie crossed her legs as she painted the witch's dress.

He stared at her for a moment. "Whatever it is,

it's not as important as spending tonight hiding away with Annie Masters."

Fire bristled in her gray eyes. "I am *not* hiding."

A popular and rich young actress left Tinseltown, joined the Army and then disappeared from public life to run an Arctic medical clinic. Even if she didn't have any interest in being in front of the camera, Annie was an excellent doctor—she could work anywhere. She might not want to call it hiding, but it certainly looked like it.

"Sorry, Annie. I guess it's just hard to think of anyone walking away from Hollywood. So many people want the glitz and the glamour."

The fact that Annie avoided all of it was fascinating. He loved stepping on stage, interacting with fans—being well-respected and important.

"You enjoy acting?"

"*The Dr. Dave Show* isn't really acting—but, yes, I enjoy it. I get to be part of people's lives." Rafe coughed. "A therapist would probably argue I'm trying to fill the hole in my soul."

"*Are* you?"

Annie leaned her head against her knees. Her gray eyes studied him, but Rafe didn't see any judgement in her expression. Maybe that was why talking to her seemed so natural. He'd always kept a part of himself from the women he dated. No one needed to know how broken he was. But Rafe wanted to tell Annie *almost* everything.

"Maybe. My mom—" Rafe coughed again.

He'd almost told Annie about his mother's abandonment—about the pain it had caused him, his desperate need to make someone—anyone— see him.

"Well, there was never enough attention to go around when I was growing up. Maybe that's why I enjoy interacting with the fans so much. They see Dr. Bradstone, a successful doctor, sitting on Dave's stage offering medical advice— not a lonely kid with no place to call home."

Annie's gray eyes bored through his soul.

"Plus, I do love standing in those lights."

Annie offered him a shy smile. "It's not bad to want those lights, Rafe." Annie bit her lip. "The image your fans see is the real you. You *are* a successful, talented, kind doctor. If they can see it, maybe you should too."

Rafe wanted to pick her up and squeeze her tight. Find the words to tell her how much that statement meant—how much all her words meant. Part of him had been knitted together that night she'd told him he was more than his parents' horrid genetics. A few others had said it, but Annie made him want to believe it.

"How about some music?"

Before he could answer Annie hustled over to a small closet. Speakers crackled on, followed by the musical tones of a song from *Les Misérables*.

"Show tunes? Dr. Annie Masters likes show tunes?"

"Of course. They tell a story."

"A sad one," Rafe joked as he moved to paint the ghost's eyes.

"Not all of them." Annie stuck her tongue out as she returned her focus to the witch.

For an hour, show tunes danced across the speakers, and Rafe tried to keep his focus on the decorations before him rather than the beauty next to him. It would have been easier if he hadn't caught her staring at him—several times.

After finishing his third candy corn, Rafe stood and marched over to the speaker system. He wanted to dance with Annie and they needed to practice, but that was secondary. Rafe wanted to hold her, and he was tired of trying to pretend the need would disappear.

"Time to dance."

* * *

As the lyrics hummed around the room Annie frowned. The Fall Carnival wasn't a real dance competition. Most people just did silly dances they'd seen on the internet or let their kids make up something fun.

"Rafe, the dance is—"

His arm slid around her waist and Annie's tongue refused to utter the truth. She wanted to stay in his arms. Let him hold her.

"So how rusty *are* you?"

"A little. But…" Annie pinched her eyes shut. "I was a child actor. My mother started me in ballet and tap as soon as I turned three. She made sure I had a diverse résumé."

Her mother had never cared if Annie actually liked the activities. Dancing, singing, violin, horseback riding were all just accomplishments that directors might like.

Annie had loved dancing, but it was families and partners who danced at the carnival. Annie didn't have either. Her stomach twisted as Rafe pulled her closer. If she wanted to, she could lean her head against his chest.

Instead she licked her lips and looked up. "I've never had a partner for the Monster Mash."

Smiling, Rafe held her gaze as he began to move them around the room. "Well, you do now, and we are going to win that ridiculous stuffed bear trophy."

Rafe's footsteps were confident as he spun her. Her heart pounded as she rolled back into his firm grasp. "Where did you learn to dance?"

"My father was a professional dancer. He taught me several things when I was little. I've taken a few classes. It was fun, but I've never had a full-time partner. No one has ever matched my steps like you do."

Sparks shot through Annie as a swing song started. "I *love* swing dancing."

Rafe's eyes lit up, and her heart pounded in her ears. Why had she put this off? The world disappeared when she was in Rafe's arms. The arguments she'd made about keeping her distance evaporated as she matched his steps.

A slow song started, and Rafe pulled Annie to his chest. Her cheeks were pink, and he felt all his barriers tumble down as she placed her head on his shoulder.

Dancing with Annie was the definition of perfection, and Rafe suspected he would never get tired of holding her.

"That trophy is as good as ours," he said.

Ours...

The word hung off Rafe's lips and he couldn't take it back. Not that it mattered; Rafe didn't want to. He'd never experienced an "ours" moment. Everything was either Rafe's or someone else's—easy to separate when relationships soured.

He desperately wanted to share that silly trophy with Annie. For a precious moment in time Rafe would belong to something so much bigger than his fans. He'd make sure the photo made it on Blue Ash's wall of memories.

Annie's forehead nuzzled against his neck as she whispered, "I think we may need more practice."

Her breath on his neck set fireworks off across Rafe's skin. He'd dance with her any time of day, in any circumstance.

"You just have to step into my arms..."

Rafe pushed a curl that had escaped from her tight ponytail away from her cheek. For a moment he feared she'd step away, but instead her full lips moved toward his.

The front door slammed shut and Annie jumped out of Rafe's arms.

"Sorry, Annie." Helen Henkle's eyes shifted

between the pair of them and the unfinished decorations.

Jack said nothing as he carried a load of boxes to the other side of the room, but his eyes held Rafe's.

"It's fine." Annie looked at her feet as she walked toward the paintbrushes. "We were just practicing. Rafe is a natural. That trophy might spend a year in the clinic."

Helen smiled as she stared at Rafe. "Is that so?"

Rafe shrugged. His arms ached without Annie, and he crossed them to keep from pulling her back to him and finishing what they both clearly wanted. "It's going to look great on the reception desk."

Thoughts kept worming their way through Annie's mind as she stared at the northern lights dancing through her skylight. Normally the peaceful sight provided her with a meditative place to sink into dreams.

Annie buried her head in her pillow. She'd almost kissed Rafe. Three times there'd been an opportunity, and she still didn't know how he kissed.

It was a dangerous thought, with no answer.

Annie enjoyed Rafe's company, but he was tied to a life in front of the camera. He loved the stage. Any person who was with Rafe would have to be part of that world. It had taken her years to carve out her own paradise away from the camera.

But Rafe was leaving. She didn't have to be part of his world if this was temporary.

The argument beat against her. She didn't want "temporary."

Sighing, she slid her feet into her panda slippers and tiptoed to the kitchen. The pint of chocolate ice cream calling to her from the refrigerator might not help her sleep, but it would make the time more enjoyable as it passed…

Freezing, Annie stared at Rafe as he lifted a spoonful of ice cream to his lips.

"Are you craving ice cream at midnight too?"

Grabbing a spoon, Annie tried to ignore the pull of need as she joined Rafe at the table. "I hope you saved some?"

Crimson stains traced his neck as he turned the empty carton toward her. "Sorry, Annie…"

"Not even a spoonful left?" Annie shook her head.

"Annie—wait," Rafe grabbed her hand, spinning her toward him. "I'm so sorry."

"It's not a huge crime, but it does mean we need more ice cream."

Annie offered him a weak smile. Ice cream wasn't what she really wanted. She thought about stepping into his arms. If they danced around the kitchen would he kiss her?

"I'll get more."

Rafe headed out of the kitchen before she could work up the courage to tell him ice cream wasn't what she craved.

"Do you know even where the ice cream is?" Had she ever told him where the clinic fridge was? Her mind was mushy with exhaustion and longing as she followed him.

"I'm sure I can find a gas station."

Annie's heart thudded as she followed him to his bedroom. "Rafe, that's a sweet offer—especially as the closest open convenience store is more than thirty miles away." She grabbed his shoes. "Luckily, I have three pints of cookie dough ice cream, two more chocolate and a rainbow sherbet I bought for reasons I cannot remember in the clinic freezer. There must have been at best six bites of ice cream left in that pint you pilfered."

"It was closer to four..." Rafe laid his keys

on the dresser and she saw his eyes wander to his bed.

Why had she followed him in here? The soft scent of sandalwood and his shampoo clawed at her senses. Her eyes kept hovering above the rumpled bed sheets.

She hugged his shoes to keep herself from stepping into his arms as she backed out of his room.

"I'll grab you another pint too."

Pain shot through her arm as she bumped it against the wall. A small cry escaped her lips, but she kept moving.

"Annie?"

She spun. "Yes?"

"If you'll hand me my shoes I'll come with you."

Desire spun across his dark eyes, but he didn't reach for her. His eyes traveled over her. It shouldn't matter, but she pulled at the sleeve of her long blue nightshirt. It wasn't an enticing outfit, but her insides burned as he studied her.

She tossed him his shoes. "Don't you trust me to bring back your goodies?"

"How do I know there aren't more flavors you don't wish to share?"

Throwing a hand across her forehead, Annie

pretended to faint. "You wound me! However, the raspberry chocolate is for special occasions, and you are to leave it alone."

Rafe's lips brushed the top of her head as he threw an arm over her shoulder. It was a friendly gesture—safe and so unsatisfying.

"So there *are* secret flavors!"

Energy danced along Annie's spine as Rafe's laughter pulsed through her. "Only the one."

At the freezer, she grabbed a pint of cookie dough and stood aside so Rafe could make his selection.

Grabbing another chocolate, Rafe snapped a quick picture with his phone.

"What are you doing?" Annie stared as he swiped a few buttons.

Rafe shrugged as he dropped the phone back in his pocket. "I haven't updated my social media much since I arrived. My large follower count is one of the leverage points my agent is using to get me a permanent position on *Dr. Dave*."

His agent—the words threw a damper on her desire. Rafe didn't belong here. He belonged to the lights and the crowds.

Back in the kitchen, her ice cream sat unopened on the table. "Have you lost many followers while you've been here?" she asked.

Guilt strode across her belly as Rafe dropped his spoon. He flinched as his phone squawked. He'd wanted the "likes," so why was he embarrassed now? Annie considered apologizing, but the words stuck on her tongue.

Rafe's foot tapped against the table and he didn't meet her gaze. "My fans are used to hearing from me a few times a day. Social media is a tricky world of algorithms and..." His voice died away.

"I'll take that non-answer as a yes." Annie blew out a breath as she pulled the lid off her ice cream. Life was so much more than a fake online presence and fans who loved you Monday and hated you Tuesday.

"Fame isn't real, Rafe. I know it can seem like it, with the intoxication of being recognized..." She stuffed the spoon into her mouth to stop the lecture. He *wanted* the fan interaction. It wasn't bad; it just wasn't the life Annie needed.

"It feels good, though. For a little while I get to belong. Without *Dr. Dave* I won't get that." Rafe laid his hand on the table, but his fingers didn't reach for hers.

Annie stared at his hand for a moment, weighing her words. It was fine to want the attention, but Rafe was looking for more than his fans could provide. "What your fans want from you isn't real belonging. They want a fantasy."

"What do *you* want?" Rafe's tongue darted across the chocolate ice cream dripping down his spoon.

You.

That declaration stayed buried as she grabbed another bite of ice cream. Finally, she continued. "I just want to be Annie. And that's not enough for many of the fans who grew up wishing to meet Charlotte Greene."

"You already have that." Rafe's fingers traced the edge of the table, so close to hers but still not touching.

"I have it in Blue Ash—not anywhere else."

Annie blew out a breath. Her chest hurt as she replayed that statement. She *wasn't* hiding in Blue Ash. Annie wanted to believe that, but—

Rafe's phone continued to ding. Apparently his late-night ice cream post was popular. He ignored it, but the outside world invaded their private haven with each buzz.

I want you. The real Rafe. The swing dancer who has a midnight sweet tooth and gets cold easily. Not the persona that makes an algorithm happy.

Annie swallowed the words as she spun her

pint of ice cream toward him and grabbed his. "My turn for the chocolate."

A smile pulled at Rafe's lips. Lifting his spoon, he laughed. "I don't want cookie dough. *En garde*, Annie."

Giggling, she defended the chocolate from the swipes of his spoon as he dove for the carton. *This* was belonging. Laughing over ice cream, late at night, with no audience. How could she make him understand?

Finally she pushed it to the middle of the table. "Guess I can share."

The bottom of the carton appeared too quickly, and Annie waved away Rafe's offer to let her have the final bite. Looking at the clock, she reluctantly pushed away from the table.

If she didn't leave now...

"Thanks for keeping me company. We have a full schedule tomorrow. I think we both need some sleep."

Annie's fingers brushed his as they reached for the empty ice cream containers at the same time. Lightning flashed between them, and suddenly Annie didn't care about the buzz of the phone, or anything else. She just wanted—needed—to know how he kissed.

"Rafe..."

Ignoring the tension racing through her belly, she leaned forward. He tasted of chocolate, heat and summer. Her heart gasped at the tender way his mouth shifted under hers, accepting her exploration.

If she took his hand, he'd come with her to bed...

The thought excited her before panic rushed into its place.

Stepping away, she stared at him. "I—"

Rafe placed a finger against her lips. "Don't apologize. Please."

Pursing her lips, she grabbed the containers, holding them before her like an empty sugar wall between her and temptation.

"I wasn't going to apologize."

Annie held her breath, wishing she had the courage to ask him to follow her and hating the uncertainty that kept the words buried.

Rafe soft lips brushed her cheek. "I'll see you tomorrow."

His words held a promise and an escape.

CHAPTER FOUR

JUST AS HIS fingers touched the blue cotton of Annie's nightshirt Rafe's alarm sounded. Wiping the sweat from his forehead, Rafe glared at his phone as he turned the alarm off. All of his dreams had involved Annie.

His body hadn't operated on so little sleep since his residency. Rolling his head, Rafe grimaced as his shoulders revolted. If the scattered bed sheets had been because Annie had spent the night in his bed Rafe wouldn't have minded the exhaustion.

The light press of her kiss had nearly driven him over the edge. Her fingers twisting along his shoulder had ignited the longing Rafe had been trying to ignore. He'd wanted to lift the light cotton separating them and kiss the line of freckles that disappeared under the nightshirt's scooped neckline. If Annie hadn't stepped away he'd have gladly stayed awake for several more hours, getting to know every inch of her.

Desire tugged at his groin and Rafe sucked in a breath. Annie had kissed him and walked away. He wanted her, but he was concerned about the connection vibrating between them. Annie was a romantic. She believed in love and the long-term. Rafe should keep his distance, but he didn't want to.

He needed to find another way to occupy his thoughts. The smell of coffee wafted through his door. Caffeine called to him as he grabbed a sweater and headed for the kitchen.

Annie yawned as she turned to greet him. Grabbing the coffee pot, Annie tipped it toward him. "I made it extra-strong. Figured we needed it after—" heat traveled up her cheeks "—after our late night."

Lightning scattered across his body when Annie's fingers brushed his. She was just passing him a coffee mug, but Rafe hoped she meant more with that small touch. His mouth watered as his eyes wandered Annie's full lips.

Those lips shook slightly, before she gestured to the cabinet. "Do you want cereal or oatmeal?"

I want you.

Rafe cleared his throat. "A donut sounds good,

but I'll settle for oatmeal." It was a dumb joke, and Rafe felt heat travel up his neck.

"Donut?"

Rafe wanted to believe Annie's brain was foggy with desire too, but his non-sequitur was surely to blame for her confusion.

Rafe winked, trying to recover from the flub. "Guess I'm just craving something sweet this morning."

Pink traveled up Annie's neck as she headed to the table. She was adorable. He wanted to kiss her. But Rafe leaned against the counter instead. "What's your favorite donut?"

It was a silly question, but he needed the answer. He wanted to know everything about Annie.

Annie hesitated. Was he really asking her about *donuts* after last night's kiss? Annie had wanted to jump into his arms this morning. Instead she'd forced herself to pour coffee and act normal. But if he was talking about pastries, then Rafe must want this morning to be like any other. That was good—but it stung.

"Are favorite donuts too personal?" Rafe teased.

"No..."

Annie ran a finger along her coffee mug. She didn't typically share details of her life. She'd spent her childhood and teen years being interviewed. When people probed it usually set off alarms in her mind. But Rafe always seemed genuinely interested in just *her*.

"I've never had a donut."

Rafe pushed his large hands through his dark hair and stared at her. What would those hands feel like running across her skin? Annie's stomach tightened with longing. A night with Rafe would be memorable, but he didn't believe in romance or love, and Annie didn't do flings. But she wanted Rafe—desperately.

Rafe's knee brushed hers as he slid into a chair. "How have you made it to adulthood and not had a double chocolate donut?"

His toffee eyes pressed against her soul.

He really wanted to know her history with pastries.

If she moved her pinky finger she'd brush his thumb.

She was in trouble…

Rafe's mouth watered, but it wasn't the oatmeal on his spoon he craved.

"Seriously, Annie, how have you managed to

avoid donuts all this time? Every TV set I've ever been on has a sweet table. It sets my eight-year-old self and my doctor self at odds every time."

A shadow passed over her eyes as she lifted her coffee mug to her lips. "I wasn't allowed to eat anything that hadn't been approved by my mother. Charlotte had to look the same each season; it didn't matter that I was growing and changing."

Rafe's jaw clenched. "How could your mom—?"

Annie flinched and Rafe bit his lip. That was a stupid question. He *knew* her mother. Carrie was responsible for his entertainment career. She was driven, but "caring" and "maternal" were not adjectives anyone would ascribe to the woman. Living with her, being unable to fire her, must have been a nightmare.

Rafe opened his mouth to say so and then clenched it shut. He hadn't told Annie that Carrie was his agent. Their introduction had gone so haywire he hadn't wanted to inflame it even more. Now the omission hung between them like a knife.

"Sorry..." Rafe's voice trailed off. He was unsure if he was apologizing for Carrie's mistakes or his own.

"You don't need to apologize." Annie squeezed his hand.

He rubbed her thumb, grateful when she didn't pull away.

"Now you know my history with pastries, are there any other secrets you want to hear?" Annie winked, but her voice wavered slightly.

"All of them. I enjoy learning about you."

"Well, I had an 'interesting' childhood…" Annie's peppy voice raced across the kitchen.

Rafe gripped her hand tighter. "You're so much more than Charlotte Greene, Annie."

Her eyes sparkled but her lips turned down. How could she not see how amazing she was?

"You, Dr. Annie Masters, are fascinating." His heart lighted as she smiled at him. "And before I leave you are going to try a double chocolate donut." Rafe ran his finger along the soft skin of her wrist before forcing himself to release her.

"We're in the Arctic, Rafe."

"Really? I thought the snow was a hologram."

The sound of Annie's giggles sent a thrill through him.

"I'll still bet there's a donut shop here!"

"And what if I hate double chocolate donuts?" she teased, laughing harder as he threw a hand over his heart.

"Then we will just have to find a donut that

calls to you. I firmly believe everyone has one that when they see it, they just have to taste it."

"Really?" Annie's eyes narrowed. "You are giving a lot of power to donuts."

Rafe's knee moved against hers as he leaned toward her. The soft scent of mint and lavender clung to her hair. Her lips were so close. He pressed his tongue to the roof of his mouth, willing the dry texture away.

"Whenever I moved to a new foster home I always found the closet donut shop. Double chocolate donuts were my dad's favorite, and on my worst days that donut always made me feel better. Donuts have a ton of power, and I refuse to believe otherwise."

Annie wrapped her fingers around his and Rafe closed his eyes. If she closed the distance between them Rafe would kiss her, run his hands through her hair... Sucking in a breath, Rafe tried to release the tension in his chest. He knew what it was like to kiss her now, and one taste hadn't been enough. Rafe suspected it would never be enough.

"I think I'd like to eat donuts with you," Annie said.

"Now I'm *definitely* going to find a donut shop."

Annie raised her coffee mug and her cheeks burned bright. "Well, let me know when you do."

Heat stormed across Annie's skin as she headed for the clinic. A conversation about donuts and she'd wanted to invite Rafe to spend the night with her. The invitation had been on the tip of her tongue.

She'd never thrown such an invitation to a partner before. She was reserved, cautious—an overthinker. She'd waited months to finally confess her attraction to Blake and lost precious time in the process.

Grabbing a stack of files from her desk, Annie toyed with the Band-Aid on her finger. Nerves warred with desire for control of her stomach. There were always going to be reasons to say no, but Annie didn't want to anymore. Tonight she was going to step into Rafe's arms and enjoy the limited amount of time they had.

A light tap against her door forced Annie's attention away from Rafe. "Dr. A?"

"Yes, Miranda?" Annie smiled at her receptionist as she stepped into the hall.

"Ms. Werth is in Room Three and she's cranky."

Tara Werth was always cranky. She'd moved

to Alaska with the oil company's first wave of employees and dated every eligible man in town before declaring Blue Ash to be devoid of culture and acceptable bachelors. Her gripes were well rehearsed and well-known. She must be extra moody for Miranda even to notice.

"Thanks for the heads-up."

She took a quick look at Tara's chart before stepping into the exam room. There wasn't anything written down under "complaints." Bracing herself, Annie stepped into the room—and dropped the chart.

"Ms. Werth? Do you need my help to close your exam gown?"

The woman's shapely derriere clenched as she turned and glared at Annie. "I thought Dr. Bradstone was going to check my mole." She crossed her arms. "I specifically told Miranda I wanted to see Dr. Bradstone."

Bending to pick up the chart, Annie barely caught back a reprimand. Tara's plan was ridiculous—the sort of scene one might watch playing out in a cheesy made-for-TV movie. Dating patients was unethical anyway. Rafe would have looked at what Annie suspected was a nonexistent mole and sent the woman on her way.

This was the price of Rafe's rising star. Dealing with excitable fans willing to act out in order to get the attention of their object of fascination. This wasn't belonging—it was fans taking, expecting him to give whatever they demanded.

Offering what she hoped was a pleasant smile, Annie walked over. "Which mole would you like me to take a look at?"

"I don't want *you* to look at any of them. You're not *him*." Spittle formed at the corners of Tara's lips as she vibrated with anger.

Annie sat on the small stool in the room and waited for Tara's fury to subside. She'd seen this behavior before—the need to get to someone you admired and fantasized about. Though that had been people trying to get to *her*.

Taking a deep breath, Annie started again. "Tara—"

"I want to see the *famous* doctor!"

Patients' demands were often unmanageable, but this was ridiculous. Annie would look at Tara's mole and then make sure Tara was not released from the room until Rafe was with a patient. She might not be able to protect Rafe from the rabid fans in LA, but in Blue Ash she could ensure he wasn't accosted at work.

"Tara, I'm happy to examine your skin, but I

will not interrupt the flow of my clinic. Now, where is this mole?"

Tara stuck her lip out, but Annie didn't waver. Finally, Tara frowned before pulling her gown up over her hip. A quarter-sized mole jutted out just below her waist.

"Obviously it's nothing," she huffed, and marched over to her clothes.

"Wait." Annie stepped closer. "I need to see that again."

"Why? It's just a dumb little mole." Tara's lip shook and a tear raced across her cheek.

"Do you have any history of skin cancer in your family?" Patting Tara's hand, Annie led her back to the exam table.

Tara's shoulders trembled as she nodded. The range of emotions patients displayed when they were scared was infinite.

"My mom had skin cancer. I've spent a lot of time in tanning beds… It's grown. I should have come in, but…"

She'd come because of Rafe. His star power had overridden Tara's fear. "Then it's a good thing you did."

Her waiting room had been packed since Rafe's arrival, but if they caught even a handful of diagnoses for patients who wouldn't have walked through her door otherwise, then Annie was grateful for his Tinseltown ties.

"I'm going to remove the mole and send a sample to the lab."

"It's *cancer*?" Tara's voice ricocheted around the room.

The word terrified everyone, but Annie needed Tara to stay calm. "It might be a basal cell carcinoma. It's a very treatable form of skin cancer. If necessary, we can use a cream to kill any other cells. I'll call with the results as soon as we have them."

Tara wiped a tear from her cheek. "Can Dr. Bradstone call me instead?"

"No." Rafe was a doctor—not public property. "Since I'm treating you, and I'm your physician of record, I'll make the call. You can feel free to contact the clinic with any questions."

Annie stepped out of the exam room and glared at the giggles echoing from the room where Rafe was seeing a patient. Pain shot along her jaw, and she forced her teeth to unclench. It wasn't Rafe's fault people were booking appointments just to meet him.

She was jealous. Her muscles tightened as the emotion ripped through her. If she wanted to explore her connection with Rafe, this was one of the prices to be paid. Did it matter that so many people vied for his attention?

Annie waited for fear or uncertainty to tumble through her, but it was excitement and longing that materialized.

It didn't matter that Rafe was extremely popular with his fans. It didn't matter that he was returning to LA or that he liked his fame. Annie needed to know what would happen if she stepped into his well-defined arms and followed through on the desire bubbling in each of them.

"Enjoying the snowstorm?"

Annie's soft scent released a little of the tension in his shoulders. "Didn't realize we were having a snowstorm," he said.

"It won't be too bad, but for the next two weeks our patient load will be pretty light. I've got snowmobiles in the garage if there's an emergency."

"Two weeks..." Rafe croaked. Winter was closer than he wanted to admit.

"These early snows always melt faster than the weathermen predict." Her lips folded as her eyes met his. "Don't worry—Jack can still fly you out if necessary."

He hated that her first thought was his escape

plan. Rafe didn't want Annie worrying about what the snow meant for *him*. He was worried about *her* winter plans. He knew Jenn was still trying to get her father situated in his retirement home.

Rafe stared at the snow piling up in the parking lot. "What if Jenn can't get here?"

The question hovered between them. Rafe wished he could pull it back. He wanted to joke about donuts or discuss musicals—not remind them both that his time in Blue Ash had an expiration date.

Annie shrugged. "Then I winter it alone—again."

Again. He hated that word. "What about Dr. Henkle? He should be here to help out."

"Liam is busy." Annie's smile faltered.

His brain flipped at her statement. "So are *you*, Annie. Doing everything yourself isn't sustainable."

Annie looked at the ceiling. "Liam can't be here full-time. He just can't."

Had they been lovers? Was that why her partner was keeping his distance? Jealousy pooled through him, and he pushed it away. Everyone had a past.

"I can't stay through the winter."

"I'm not asking you to!" She threw her hands in the air.

The pain rolling through Rafe surprised him. He should be *glad* she wasn't demanding more than he could give—that he didn't have to disappoint her. Except he wanted to be able to make Annie promises.

"I'm sorry. I shouldn't probe about your clinic staffing. You've run this place through four winters."

Alone.

"I appreciate the concern. I really do." Annie's eyes darted to the falling snow. "This wasn't how tonight was supposed to start."

Annie's sigh punched at him. He'd wanted tonight to start differently too. "I'm worried about you. You shouldn't be alone."

Rafe stepped forward, praying she wouldn't retreat.

"What about you?" Annie stepped closer. "Despite all those fans you're alone."

Rafe ran a finger along her chin. "I don't feel alone when I'm with you."

"I'm glad." Annie stepped into his arms.

Everything shifted as he closed the distance between their lips. Annie had kissed Rafe last night; now he kissed her.

Her soft lips opened and Rafe thought his senses would explode. Running his fingers along her back, Rafe lost himself in the subtle sighs echoing from Annie. Blood pounded in his ears. He wanted nothing more than to race upstairs, but he'd arranged a surprise for her.

"I have something for you."

Rafe had asked one of his patients where to get donuts. The sweet woman had recommended he call Annie's baker friend, Holly. She'd personally delivered her favorite dozen during her lunch break.

Small lines danced at the corner of her lips as Annie smiled. "You do?" Her eyes sparked with anticipation as she placed a light kiss against Rafe's jaw. "Why don't we look at it upstairs?"

"I'll grab it from the back and meet you there."

Rafe's heart raced as Annie smiled at him.

Holding the donuts, he climbed the stairs to the apartment two at a time. Tonight held so much promise.

Rafe hesitated in the kitchen. "Annie?"

"I'm in my room. Come on—the show is about to start."

Rafe held his breath as he stepped across the threshold of Annie's private sanctuary. This was not a place she invited people, and Rafe was humbled that she wanted him here.

The room was huge—larger than any of the studio apartments he'd lived in since moving to LA. A large blanket was lain across the floor, and Rafe's heart felt like it wanted to explode as he gazed at the massive skylight. His body tensed with longing as he moved his eyes away from her iron post bed with its homey pink-and-gray quilt.

Rafe set the donuts on the bright purple chest decorated with sunflowers at the end of her bed. "This is unique," Rafe said, as he slid the top off the box.

"Unique?" Annie laughed as she crossed her legs. "I made it. Everyone needs a winter hobby. Mine is repurposing furniture—usually in bright colors! I can smell sweetness from here; did you buy dessert for the show?"

Rafe turned his head, looking for a television. "You want to watch a movie?"

"No! In about ten minutes the northern lights are going to dance across that skylight."

Rafe smiled as he placed one of the donuts on the plate Holly had kindly included. "I promised you a double chocolate donut."

A slow smile spread across Annie's face as

she stared at the gooey pile. "You bought me donuts?"

"Yep. For future reference, your friend Holly doesn't just make cookies and cakes. Something you might learn, if you spent a bit more time away from the clinic."

Rafe hurried on, not wanting to start another spat, "Holly was very impressed I was wooing you with donuts."

Annie's hands hovered over the box. "Wooing me with donuts? You *are* a romantic."

Leaning across the blanket, Rafe pressed his lips to the soft dimple in her cheek. He liked that Annie thought he was a romantic, but it wasn't true. He didn't want to give her expectations.

"It's just donuts, Annie. Romance is grand gestures and sweeping statements." He was only offering a donut.

Staring at the donut, Annie laughed. "You're wrong. Romance is the little things." Tearing the donut, Annie handed him half. "You, Dr. Rafe Bradstone, are a romantic."

Rafe raised an eyebrow but didn't argue. He suspected anyone Annie let get close would want to do things for her. It was impossible not to fall under her spell.

"To donuts on a blanket, under the northern lights, with great company."

As she bit into the donut Annie's eyes lit up. "Oh, that is *good*." Annie leaned her head against his chest and sighed. "Thank you, Rafe."

"Anytime."

Running his fingers along her shoulder, Rafe smiled. He'd waited all day for this quiet moment with Annie. This moment—her sitting in his arms eating a donut—was one Rafe suspected he'd spend the rest of his life replaying. Leaning closer, he inhaled the soft scent of chocolate and lavender cascading off her. If there was a better place to be than the Arctic with Dr. Annie Masters, he wasn't sure he wanted to find it.

"Rafe…"

His name on her lips sent need racing through him. Swallowing, Rafe let his eyes linger on her soft mouth for only a moment before meeting her gaze.

"Yes?"

"Kiss me."

The simple request nearly undid him.

The sky lit up as his lips met hers. Blues and greens burst through the skylight as Annie ran her hands along the base of his neck.

"Rafe…"

She tasted of chocolate, sugar and simply Annie. His name on her lips sent waves of need cascading through him. Rafe pulled her into his lap, let his hands stroke the back of her neck before he moved to undo the tight bun she always wore.

Annie pulled back, doubt crossing her eyes. Rafe sucked in a ragged breath. He wanted her, but if she had any doubts...

"Annie, if you want to watch the lights—"

Her hands trembled as she reached for the rubber band. "My curls are crazy. My hairdresser used to spend two hours straightening them when I played Charlotte." Tight curls sprang from their confines, cascading past her shoulders. "Everyone expects—"

He captured her statement with his mouth. Rafe didn't care about Charlotte. Didn't want that name lingering between them.

"You're gorgeous, *Annie*."

Tonight, there was only Rafe and Annie. Her fictional character was a cardboard illustration compared to the woman before him.

Annie smiled, but he could see that Charlotte's ghost clung to her.

Pulling her hand across his stomach, Rafe kissed her cheek and waited until her eyes met his. "It's *you* I want touching me. The woman who helped me with Mac's leg and joked about superhero undies, who told me I needed new shoes if I didn't want to lose my toes, who decorated that bright purple-and-yellow chest and who I watched devour her first donut. It's *you*, Annie."

Annie placed her hands on either side of Rafe's face and urged him to kiss her. Demanded it. And he was more than willing to oblige.

Gripping her butt, Rafe fell into the kiss. Dipping his head, he traced her neck with his tongue before turning his attention to the buttons of her shirt. He kissed each inch of skin that appeared as he pushed her shirt to the floor. He skimmed the line of freckles dotting the tops of her breasts.

"You are amazing, Annie..."

As Rafe turned his attention to her full round breasts, Annie felt the room start to shake.

Worry transited her veins, but the small earth tremors that were a monthly occurrence here didn't really bother her.

Rafe—she could fall for him. A part of her already had...

Annie's thoughts were jumbled as Rafe's soft lips captured hers.

Her pictures clacked against the wall and the building creaked as the room swayed. Was the earth celebrating this union or warning her?

Annie threw off the random thought as Rafe's heat melted through her. And as they melded together Annie's worries floated away. She wanted him—even if it was only for tonight.

Annie wrapped her arms around Rafe's shoulders as the earth shook. His fingers gripped her hips.

"Was that an earthquake?"

Annie grinned. "Don't you live in California?"

"Yes—but, in case you haven't noticed the snow and extreme cold, this isn't California."

Fire exploded across her skin as Rafe's lips trailed along the top of her breasts.

No, it wasn't California.

Running her fingers along the zipper of his jeans, Annie felt her stomach flutter when his breath hitched. "There was a tremor the day you arrived too. Were you so taken with finding me you didn't notice?"

Rafe nipped her shoulder. "I was, and still am, *very* taken with you."

His fingers slid down her back. He unhooked her bra and sat up. His dark eyes swept across her body, but he didn't touch her. Panic traced up Annie's spine as he stared at her. Was she not what he'd expected...wanted?

"You are perfect."

Her lips trembled at the simple statement. She wasn't sure it was true, but she appreciated the words.

"Glad you like freckles."

Rafe's brows furrowed, and then he gripped her buttocks, lifting them both as he stood.

"Rafe!"

Gentle fingers laid her across the bed. "I like everything about you, Annie." Rafe's head dipped as he licked the top of her chest. His fingers swept along the top of her jeans. "You are exquisite."

He grazed the delicate skin along her belly while he unzipped her jeans. Then, kneeling beside the bed, he pulled her to the edge.

Annie sat up and reached for him, but Rafe shook his head. "I've spent far too many minutes wondering what you taste like, and now I plan to find out."

"Rafe..." Her breath caught as his teeth nipped the soft skin of her thighs.

Rising, his lips captured her moans. "We have all night, and I plan to savor you."

Feather kisses sent tiny shocks across her skin,

but it wasn't enough. Her body burned, pulsed with desire. "Please…"

Hovering over her stomach, Rafe chuckled as Annie pressed her hips against him. "Demanding? I like that."

She wasn't normally demanding, but Rafe had unleashed an unexpected delightful wantonness in her. Cool air caressed her butt as Rafe removed her lacy panties. She quivered as he nuzzled her, his mouth teasing her, driving her closer to the edge. When his tongue dipped into her Annie wrapped her legs around him.

"Sweet, succulent and perfect."

Pleasure rocketed through her as Rafe drove her over the edge. It still wasn't enough.

Annie's hands ruffled his hair. "I need you, Rafe. *All* of you—please!"

Rafe quickly deposited his clothes on the floor. He'd never seen a sexier sight than Annie's closed eyes when she finally surrendered. She was perfect…and his—at least for tonight.

"I need you…"

Her breathy words broke him. Quickly sheathing himself, Rafe pulled her to the edge of the bed and drove home. She met his thrusts, demanding more, but he refused to hurry.

Gripping her hips, he forced their pace to slow. "I'm not rushing this."

Rafe held Annie's gaze as he thrust. Her eyes were dilated, and her ankles dug into his tight buttocks as Rafe bent his head to capture a rose-colored nipple between his lips.

Her fingers dug into his shoulders. "Rafe…"

Annie's body convulsed around him, but he refused to adjust his pace. If he lived to be a hundred Rafe doubted there would be a better sound than his name as Annie climaxed.

Her lips caressed his shoulder and a growl of desire echoed through him. Finally, he gave in to his own need. Annie's hips met his as he drove into her, and waves of heat and need pulsated through him as she crested over pleasure's edge a final time. And then reason turned to oblivion as Annie clung to him. At last, Rafe let himself join her.

Annie sucked in a deep breath. "That was—"

He loved the pink blush traveling up her cheeks as she stared at him.

When she didn't elaborate Rafe pressed. "Yes?"

Annie laughed. "I have no words."

He chuckled at her quiet statement but didn't argue. Tonight had been simply perfection.

CHAPTER FIVE

ANNIE'S FINGERS TRACED Rafe's shoulder blade before she placed a light kiss against his back. Careful not to wake him, she rolled over. Her eyes wandered across the ceiling as she tried to convince herself she'd be okay when he left. Last night had been amazing, but that didn't have to mean anything. They had a connection, an attraction, something they each wanted to explore.

Annie was lying to herself—and it wasn't even a good lie. She cared for Rafe—and not in a temporary "say goodbye in a few weeks" fling way.

She hadn't felt this way since Blake, and she hadn't gotten the chance to spend forever with Blake. Was she willing to risk her heart with Rafe?

She'd already risked it—except in the morning light everything might change.

There hadn't been many men in her life. The two she'd gotten close to since Blake's death had ended the relationship soon after they'd slept with her. Everyone went to bed with Charlotte Greene and woke next to crazy-haired, freckled Annie Masters.

She didn't want to believe it would happen with Rafe, but as his soft snores hit her back she slipped from the bed. It was a cowardly retreat, but she couldn't bear to see his face if that shift happened.

Pulling on some torn jeans and a flannel shirt, she walked into her living room. Taking the picture of Blake and Liam off the shelf, she ran her fingers across Blake's soft smile. She'd always love him. It felt wrong that she hadn't told Rafe that part of her heart was already gone. Would he still want her if he knew she'd always love another?

"Who's that?" Rafe's deep voice rolled through her as he slipped his arms around her. He pressed a kiss to her shoulder.

"That's Liam and his brother, Blake." Annie looked up at him and kissed his cheek.

"Blake? Your friend from the Army."

Friend. That title was inaccurate and her stomach twisted. She hadn't meant to downplay their relationship.

Her mouth was dry, but she managed to force

out, "Liam is Blake's brother, and Helen and Jack are his parents."

Rafe tightened his fingers along her shoulder. "You came to Alaska after he died?"

She set the photo down before turning in Rafe's arms. If he didn't understand it would be better for her to find out now. Annie hated digging into this part of her past but keeping this information from Rafe was wrong. She loved Blake and she wasn't going to hide that.

"This was Blake and Liam's land—their home. They thought it would make an excellent clinic. They were worried about the lack of medical personnel in this region of the Arctic."

"Blake joined the Army and planned to head to med school after serving his tour. I promised to help him get the clinic off the ground."

The Army had brought them together, and then it had ripped them apart.

"You loved him."

Rafe kissed the top of her forehead, but there was an emotion hovering in his eyes that she couldn't place.

"Yes. Blake made me believe I was more than Charlotte Greene."

So do you.

She sucked in a breath. Blake's loss had devastated her, but time had healed most of the wound.

"Blake was my best friend and my fiancé. He died in combat the week after he proposed."

"Fiancé?"

Rafe's voice was strained, but he didn't let go of her. She leaned her head against his shoulder. Blake was her past, but if she wanted a future with Rafe—even a temporary one—he deserved to know this.

"I should have told you."

Looking up, she met Rafe's gaze, willing him to say something.

"Is this why you left our bed?" he asked. His finger trembled as it ran along her cheek.

Our bed...

The words sent a shiver of delight down her legs. She wanted an "ours" with Rafe. She was in trouble—serious trouble.

"Did you run from me this morning?"

She couldn't force the words out, so she nodded, hating the flash of pain falling across his face.

Rafe's heart shattered as he looked at Annie's freckles. "If you don't want to continue our relationship, I understand," he said, but his words died as he ran a hand through his hair.

He stared at the smiling man in the picture on the shelf. He couldn't live up to him. He had become a doctor for all the wrong reasons. He chased the spotlight while Blake had served his country—sacrificed everything. He was the hero Annie described when she talked about love.

Annie wrapped her arms around his neck. "I—I want to wake in your arms tomorrow. I just needed you to know about Blake. I know this is temporary, but it felt wrong that I hadn't told you."

Temporary—he hated that word. But it was good that she wasn't counting on him. He wasn't Blake…wasn't forever.

"I'm glad you told me. He was a lucky man."

His phone rang. The interruption brought his life in LA to the forefront. Rafe pulled it out of his pocket and silenced it.

"Do you need to get that?" Annie asked.

"I can call my agent back anytime."

Annie frowned and stepped away. Just the word was enough to make her pull away from him. But Rafe knew her thoughts on Hollywood—it shouldn't sting.

"You didn't look—"

"She's the only one who calls me, Annie."

The sad statement ripped from him. No one called him.

Annie pulled his phone out of his pocket and slapped it into his hand. "Put my number in."

"What?"

Annie rolled her eyes and tapped his phone. "Put my number in. Your agent isn't going to be the only one calling you, Rafe. Not anymore." She kissed the tip of his nose before heading to the kitchen. "Call her back while I make coffee."

Rafe stared at the photo of Blake and Liam for several more minutes. Annie had come to Alaska to fulfill a promise to her fiancé. She wasn't hiding in this remote location. She was serving it in the place of a local man, a man she'd loved who'd never come home.

Rocking on his heels, Rafe tried to determine the emotions swirling through him. Annie still loved Blake and she always would. That didn't bother Rafe, but what if he wasn't worthy of her? If he opened his heart to her, would she accept all the baggage he carried? Annie deserved the best. Rafe knew that wasn't him, but he didn't want to walk away.

His phone rang again, and Rafe glared at the reminder of his other life. The glow of the cameras and the excitement he felt on stage were amazing. He wanted to believe there was a way to have both. But—

The phone buzzed again and he finally answered. "Carrie—"

Before he could get more out, his agent launched into a well-rehearsed script, "Rafe, we have a problem. Dave is demanding each of the hosts being considered for promotion to full-time host give him an interview. I've already worked out the details. We'll get a crew up there—a remote wilderness location is an interesting topic...much more intriguing than what Dr. Milo and Dr. Dean have planned. I already spoke with Dave, and he loves the idea. The job is as good as yours!"

"Wait."

Chills cascaded through him. Annie had walked away from Hollywood. He wasn't bringing those lights here.

"When does the interview have to be done?"

Carrie's silence dragged and Rafe smiled.

"Your silence speaks volumes."

He would postpone it—at least until he got back to LA. His ratings were significantly higher than the other potential hires; he didn't need the remote wilderness.

Bile raked across his tongue as he stared at

Blake's image. He couldn't ask Annie to give up Blake's dream for Hollywood's shallowness. But he'd spent the last several years working toward a permanent position on *Dr. Dave.* If he gave it up he'd have nothing when Annie realized he wasn't enough for her. If he gambled on chemistry and lost…

Swallowing the lump at the back of his throat, Rafe vowed he'd make the most of their temporary time.

"Rafe! If you want this job then you'll do this interview now—before the others do. The other doctors are basing their shoots in LA. You'll be the only one with the sexy Arctic wilderness. It's what Dave wants."

He flinched as Carrie's sharp rebuke echoed in his ear. Staring at the ceiling, he tried to slow the creep of unease worming through his belly. "Sexy Arctic wilderness…" That wasn't what Annie's clinic was.

"Rafe, you've spent the last two years proving yourself to Dave," Carrie hissed. "He's going to offer you the permanent position. I'm certain of it." His agent paused for a moment, and her voice was softer when she offered, "Don't throw it away."

Sinking into the couch, Rafe ran his hands

through his hair. This was more than Annie's clinic and her home—it was her mission. He couldn't ask her to give up her privacy so that he got a promotion.

"The clinic I'm at isn't really interested in publicity."

Carrie hesitated for a moment, and he heard her breathing hitched on the line before her falsetto cracked over the phone. "Dave wants an in-depth look at Arctic wilderness medicine and lots of snow. If you sell it to Annie as advancing remote medicine and the need for rural practitioners she'll do it."

Rafe though he might be ill. This morning was too full of revelations. "You know I'm in Blue Ash."

"The two social media posts you've done have location tags in Blue Ash." Carrie's sharp statement cut across the line.

"After you ran away to Tennessee for four weeks last year, it seemed prudent to keep track of you."

"I didn't run away."

Rafe pulled at a loose thread on his jeans. He'd chased a dream in Tennessee, and it had gone up in smoke. He wasn't going to lose his chance at the promotion now.

Looking out the window, he stared at the snow-flakes pouring down. "*If* I ask Annie to partici-pate—and I am not promising—Dave needs to understand this is a state-of-the-art clinic. We can talk about remote medicine and doctor short-ages, but I won't downplay the amazing work she's done here."

"How *is* my daughter?"

Rafe buried his head in his hands. Carrie's quiet question held so many others as Rafe tried to force air into his lungs. He'd never told Annie about his agent being her mom. His other life hadn't seemed to matter much. But he knew it was more than that. He hadn't trusted her to ac-cept it. Now he didn't know how to tell her with-out driving her away.

Blowing out a breath, he stumbled over his words. "Would Annie want me to answer that?"

"No." His agent's voice—Annie's mother's voice—cracked as she sucked in a rough breath. "Maybe you should have taken another vacation to Tennessee instead of heading to the Arctic. Dave really wants the northern story now."

Carrie didn't know about what had happened in Tennessee, but her statement tore through him. "Well, I'm not in Tennessee!"

Rafe slammed the phone to the floor, not caring that he hadn't said goodbye.

"What's in Tennessee?" Annie looked concerned as she stood in the doorway.

How much had she heard?

"Nothing is in Tennessee!"

A frown tripped across her face. *He'd* done that, and he hated it. But it wasn't a lie—nothing *was* in Tennessee…at least not for him.

Why hadn't he told her about Carrie? Rafe wanted to flay his earlier self. That single omission threatened everything now.

He tried to force words out, but his tongue refused to move. "I…uh… I…need to see to a few things in my room." That wasn't what he'd meant to say.

"Of course." Annie's voice was barely audible.

She didn't stop him as he pushed past her. Not that he blamed her. Annie had shared an important part of her past with him this morning and he'd walked away. If he wanted another reason to see how he didn't measure up to her former love, there it was.

Boxes were scattered across the reception area when Rafe finally found his way downstairs. A smiling ghoul hovered over the reception desk and a cauldron full of sugar-free candy had materialized by the door. His clinic in LA didn't bother with Halloween decorations; it was the same sterile beige walls and flowerpot pictures no matter the season.

Annie was hanging pumpkin string lights along the outer edges of the room. The tight pull of her shoulders made his heart ache. He'd hurt her. There was so much he needed to say.

"Annie, I'm sorry. I shouldn't have snapped at you."

"We all have things we don't want to talk about."

Holding up the strand of lights, he swallowed. This wasn't a tale he'd ever divulged. "Maybe but—" He coughed as she stepped off the step ladder.

"You don't owe me an explanation."

"I do." *For so many things.* Gesturing to a box, he tried to work up his courage. "What can I help with?"

"Those cobwebs need hanging on the windows." She pointed to the white pile of fluff on the floor beside her. "And there are pretend spiders in one of those boxes to add to them."

Twisting a cobweb through his fingers, Rafe stared at the spiders. "You told me about Blake, to give me the option of walking away. But you aren't the only one with baggage that changes things."

"Vanessa?" Annie tilted her head. "Rafe, I don't care about those tabloid headlines."

"Vanessa is an ex. We all have those. I meant my parents. The reason I need the attention you abhor."

Rafe sucked in a breath and then began.

"My mom was in Tennessee…" Tears coated his eyes and he clenched his fists. He was *not* going to shed any tears over that woman. "Actually, she still is in Tennessee. I think." He wrapped the cobweb around a nail on the window seal.

"She's still alive?"

The pumpkin lanterns trembled in Annie's hands as she stared at him. What would she think of him after he told her his own mother hadn't believed him worthy of love?

Rafe watched a few snowflakes melt against the window before he nodded. "Yeah. My dad died in a car accident when I was seven." He pushed a few spiders into the web before turning around. "Mom supported him while he chased his dreams of being a dancer. He cheated on her. Despite his cheating, she never left him. I remember her screaming at him how much she loved him, begging him to stay. She turned hard as glass when she found out he'd died in a car with her best friend. They'd been having an affair for months, apparently."

"Wow."

"Yeah—it's the stuff of TV movies." Rafe didn't try to stop the bitter laugh tumbling from his lips. "I look just like my dad. I act like him too—my walk and the way I talk. He used to call me his mini me."

He'd taken the burden of all the rage his mother hadn't been able to use on his father. All his small misdemeanors had resulted in long lectures on how he'd eventually be a liar and a womanizer.

"After he died she couldn't look at me. I used to scream at her, but she looked right past me."

Annie pulled the web from his hands. "She put you in foster care?"

He closed his eyes, hating the tear sliding down his cheek. "After he passed she stopped taking care of me. When Social Services were called in she didn't even fight for me."

Annie's arms were wrapped around his waist, and he drew strength from her heat.

"Despite that, I always thought it was a mistake. That she'd looked for me, but the authorities wouldn't tell her where I was. I had quite the fantasy life—most kids in the system do. Easier to pretend our parents miss us. I guess some do, but not mine."

Rafe inhaled the soft scent of Annie's hair. Would she still hold him like this when he told her about his connection to her mom?

Burying that fear, he continued, "I made the mistake of tracking her down via social media last year. I should have reached out on the internet, but in my head I thought our reunion would be better if I just showed up. That's how the movies play out. Everyone gets their happy ending, right?"

"Fiction is often nicer than the real world." Annie squeezed him before kissing his cheek.

Laying his head on top of hers, Rafe watched the snow fall as he went on. "I honestly assumed she'd be happy to see me."

Rafe's chest clenched as he reached the end of his story. His mother didn't want him. Thought he was unworthy. How could anyone see worth in him if his parent couldn't?

"She *should* have been happy to see you. Proud of the man you've become." Annie placed a light kiss along his cheek as she laid her hand against his heart. "It's her failing if she wasn't—not yours."

The tension in Rafe's shoulders relaxed as he wrapped his arms around Annie. She'd seen the good in him. A burden lifted off his heart as he stared into Annie's welcoming gaze. The rest of the story tumbled forth, but the bitterness coating it had dissipated.

"I'd played our reunion out in my head so many times." He had bounced outside her door, excited for what he had known was going to be an amazing day. "Instead, she ordered me off her porch, hissing that her new family didn't know I existed."

Rafe laid his head against Annie's curls. Opening up to her seemed so easy.

"Seems I look even more like my dad now. Before slamming the door in my face, she told me I was better off alone. That all the men in my family were users and incapable of love."

"That was a bitter hateful thing for her to say, and it was a lie." Annie's lips met his, their softness molding against them. "You are *not* responsible for your parents' faults."

"I know your mom." His words squeaked out.

"I think *everyone* knows my mom." Annie's smile was brittle as she squeezed him.

"Annie—"

She laid a finger over Rafe's lips. "Please. I don't want to talk about my mother. I'm too busy convincing a very handsome doctor that he is so much more than the awful words flung at him."

Annie's fingers pressed against his chin, and she laid her head against his chest.

"Don't let your mother's venom poison your future."

Hope pushed against Rafe's heart. Maybe someone *could* love him. He'd convinced himself he didn't need love—that the emotion didn't exist. What if he was wrong?

Holding Annie, Rafe felt his heart overriding his mind's objections. Maybe Annie—

His phone buzzed and the tiny bubble popped. Again Rafe had failed to tell Annie her mother was his agent. His brain screamed that he was a coward.

But he wanted to believe Annie. Wanted to think that there was a place for him on her shelf and in her life. But Rafe knew he wasn't worth keeping. His mother, Vanessa, countless foster families… No one had ever wanted to keep him. Eventually Annie wouldn't want him around either.

They'd already discussed Blake and his mother

this morning. He'd find a better time to tell her about Carrie. But that interview was not happening in Blue Ash. It would happen in LA if he couldn't find another "exotic" location for Dave. Rafe was *not* bringing cameras to Annie's clinic. No promotion was worth destroying her serene home.

CHAPTER SIX

Rafe smiled at Annie as she dropped one patient's record off and grabbed another. The past few days had been blissful. He'd briefly worried that working together would be awkward after they'd begun dating, but it actually made the day so much better.

They started the day with breakfast, went over patient's records, and Annie often shared little notes to make his patient interactions easier. At lunch they grabbed a quick sandwich in the main office, usually while finishing up morning patient notations, and then they met up for dinner.

The schedule already felt familiar—and perfect.

Now he had one final patient, and then he could spend the rest of his evening laughing, talking and making love to Annie before starting the wonderful cycle over again tomorrow.

Stepping into the exam room, Rafe held out his hand. "Good afternoon, I'm Dr. Bradstone."

"Amelia Clarke." The woman's cheeks flushed as she gripped Rafe's hand. "I can't believe I get to meet a famous person!" She squealed, and then immediately started coughing.

Rafe nodded. He'd run into several exuberant fans since his arrival in Blue Ash. They saw Annie regularly too, but no one seemed to react to her the same way. "Well, why don't you let me check that cough?"

Amelia waved a hand. "It's nothing. I came because my ear hurts."

Rafe frowned. Her cough sounded painful, but she'd turned her head and was pointing at her ear. He'd start with her complaint, but he was going to listen to her chest too.

Her eardrum was inflamed and pulsing. "Your right ear is infected," he told her. "Now I want to listen to your lungs."

"I'm just not as young as I was, Dr. Bradstone. I've had this cough for a few weeks. It will go away. Really."

She started to hop off the table but Rafe put his hand up. "Humor me." He held up the stethoscope and smiled.

Amelia sighed but acquiesced.

Her lungs were raspy. Rafe suspected she had walking pneumonia. The ear infection might be related, but it was more likely her body was trying to fight the pneumonia and hadn't been able to battle the dual infection.

Rafe pulled up a chair and folded his arms. "Mrs. Clarke—"

"Please call me Amelia."

"Amelia." Rafe smiled—everyone in Blue Ash insisted on first names. He liked that; it made him feel closer to Annie's patients. "I think you may have walking pneumonia. I need to schedule a chest X-ray to confirm. The clinic is closing now, but come in first thing tomorrow. Until then, I'm going to start you on some antibiotics for the ear infection."

Amelia frowned as she held his gaze. "Well, at least I'll get to tell my canasta group that a real celebrity checked me out twice."

Rafe laughed. "You've been checked by Dr. A before. Even though she hasn't acted in years, she's still more famous than me."

"Yes, but Dr. A is *family*. Family doesn't count for famous." She chuckled before coughing again.

"Family?" Rafe asked. He'd thought Carrie was the only relation Annie had.

Amelia smiled, but it didn't quite reach her eyes as she patted his knee. "I taught her fiancé

Blake in high school. He was such a smart boy. I never had children of my own, so I adopted all my students. Blake loved Annie, so that makes her family too. I didn't see them together, but she turned his dream into a beautiful legacy so they must have been wonderful."

Rafe's chest was heavy as he wrote out the order for an X-ray. Emotions raced through him and he had a hard time catching his breath.

"That is lovely." He knew his voice sounded stilted, but Amelia didn't seem to notice.

"I tried setting Annie up with my nephew when she moved to town. They went on two dates, but I think that was just to humor me. Colin said she was polite, but clearly not interested. Some people only love once."

Rafe swallowed as he stood. *Love*. That emotion didn't have a place in his world. So why did the thought that Annie might be incapable of loving someone else tear through him?

Amelia grabbed the paper from his hand. "Look at me…gibbering on." She shook his hand and headed for the door.

Rafe didn't follow. Looking around the room, Rafe sighed. This clinic, and the work Annie was doing here, was impressive. It was a testament to her love for Blake, ensuring his legacy.

What was Rafe's legacy? The uncomfortable question rolled through him.

If he died today, people would have only You-Tube videos and social media posts. Nothing that matched the scale of a clinic providing medicine to an underserved community.

"There you are." Annie pecked his cheek as she stepped up beside him. "Amelia has scheduled her X-ray for tomorrow before we officially open, so our shift is starting early." She bumped his hip. "Earth to Rafe?"

He placed a kiss against her forehead. "Sorry, I guess my mind is wandering."

Heat ripped up his arms as Annie wrapped her fingers through his.

"Where was it wandering?"

"Nowhere important." Rafe squeezed her tightly.

"Rafe?" A line appeared across Annie's forehead. "What's wrong?"

Brushing his lips against hers, Rafe smiled. "Nothing, sweetheart. Promise. I just got lost in thought at the end of a long day." Tapping her nose, Rafe winked. "We've been seeing patients for over ten hours. How do you keep up this schedule?"

Annie laughed, but the worry line didn't move.

"You get used to it." Pulling him toward the door, Annie squeezed his hand. "Let's order in."

"Sounds good."

Rafe wrapped his arm around Annie's waist. He had to leave in a few weeks—it didn't matter that Blake had been her one true love or that Rafe's legacy was a daytime talk show. *It didn't.*

The pillow was cold against Annie's hand when she reached for Rafe. Sitting up, she rubbed at her eyes and glared at the clock on her phone. It was a few minutes before five—where was he?

She shivered as her feet hit the cool floor. Grabbing her robe, she padded to the kitchen. It was empty.

Frowning, she headed for the guest room. Rafe hadn't used it in two weeks. If he'd left their bed for—

Her stomach clenched as she pushed the door open. She was not going to worry. *She wasn't.*

Panic rippled down Annie's back as she stared at the empty room.

"Rafe?" The name echoed in the hallway, but no answer floated back.

Racing for the clinic door, Annie tried to calm her hammering heart. Rafe wouldn't leave without telling her. She was overreacting.

But she couldn't seem to catch her breath.

The clinic was quiet, but a light in her office showed under the door. Taking a deep breath, Annie wanted to slap herself. Rafe was fine and her overreaction was ridiculous.

Swallowing, Annie considered going back up to their room. *Their* room? When had her sanctuary become theirs?

The moment she'd invited him to spend the night.

Her heart squeezed as that truth hit her and she walked toward her office. Whatever time they had left, she wanted to spend it with him.

Rafe was staring at the computer and furiously writing notes. His full lips were pursed as he read something on the screen.

Leaning against the door, Annie drank in his image. Need coated her nerves as she stared at his mussed hair and the stubble coating his chin. He was perfect.

His lips parted as he finally raised his eyes and saw her in the doorway. "Annie?"

"Nope. I'm a sleepy snow nymph who's come searching for her partner." She laughed as she dropped a light kiss against his lips. "If you're so tired that you don't recognize me in the doorway, maybe you shouldn't sneak from our bed so early in the morning."

She yelped as he pulled her into his lap.

"Rafe…" Annie moaned as the rough stubble along his chin rubbed against the sensitive skin at the base of her neck.

His hands locked around her waist. "Sorry, Annie. Stephen Donovan is having some issues. Dave wants an interview that Stephen doesn't think is a good idea. He's sent me the research—asked me to take a look and give my opinion to Dave."

"Isn't Dr. Donovan a full-time host? Why wouldn't Dave listen to him?" Annie shifted in Rafe's lap so she had a better view of the computer screen.

Rafe's fingers tapped a few keys and he pulled up an academic study. "They got into an argument a few seasons ago—before I came on board. Every so often I get a request from one of the other doctors to talk Dave out of a crazy segment. He usually listens to me—not sure why."

Rafe highlighted a few things on the screen. "Stephen sent me a panicked text a little before three. I didn't mean to wake up so early. Apparently, Dave wants to cover hot yoga and its benefits for cystic fibrosis."

"What?" Annie turned her focus from Rafe's sexy features to the screen. "Is there any scientific support for this?"

"From the research I found—minimal. It could also cause harm if the studio isn't clean. I shot off a few emails this morning to Dave and the producers, suggesting it was a poor topic. Hopefully they'll listen." Rafe's fingers slipped up her spine.

"I never realized you did so much for the show."

She'd assumed it was just an avenue for attention—a chance to stand onstage. That was what Rafe had said. But clearly it was so much more. It mattered to him.

"It's not a giant legacy, but it's the most important thing to *me*."

"Legacy?" Annie's voice was tight as her brain focused on his final statement. The show was the most important thing to Rafe?

What else would it be?

Rafe's lips trailed light kisses down her neck. "Weird word to assign to a daytime talk show, I know."

Rafe chuckled, but the tone of it was off. There was something he wasn't telling her.

"People listen to Dave," she said. "They believe the things he tells them because he has a show and wears a white lab coat. If you're keeping phony science off the air, you're helping keep the viewers safe. That is a noble thing, Rafe."

"Maybe."

But his eyes narrowed as they held hers. He didn't believe her.

"Rafe—"

Before she could argue more, he captured her lips.

CHAPTER SEVEN

STRONG ARMS WRAPPED around Annie's waist and a light snore echoed in her ear as the first hint of sun poured through her skylight. Turning, she drank in Rafe's features, softened in sleep. Annie pressed her lips to his. Heat pooled on her skin as his hand skimmed along the top of her butt.

"I didn't mean to wake you…" Annie kissed his chin.

"Hmm…" Rafe's lips found her neck as his fingers traced her inner thigh. "I think you did."

He rubbed his chin along her clavicle, the bristles raking her delicate skin. Annie let her fingers trail his hard length as her body quivered.

"If stubble is such a turn-on, I may need to grow a beard."

Kissing the top of his head, Annie inhaled the soft scent of his shampoo. "I wouldn't mind that."

She sighed as his mouth found her nipple. This

had been their routine for the last two weeks. It was perfect—and that was the problem.

Annie ran her hands down Rafe's back, trying to push the bubble of fear away. These last few weeks were ingrained in her soul. A piece of her was attached to Rafe, and she didn't know what that meant. She'd always love Blake, but he'd gone where she couldn't follow. And Rafe was heading back to LA.

She wanted to believe they could find a way to move forward—Rafe was only going to be a few plane trips away—but they never talked about the future. Instead, they were cramming a lifetime into just weeks. They fell asleep in each other's arms, woke together, made love and pretended the passing days didn't mean anything.

She lifted her thigh over his. "Rafe…" His name sounded like a prayer as he slipped inside her.

Rafe rocked them. There was no rush for orgasm, just the need to be as one. She thought her heart might explode.

"I think I could spend an eternity touching you and still never trace each of your freckles."

Rafe's lips tripped along her nose before capturing her inevitable rebuttal. How did he make the flaws she saw seem gorgeous?

Pressure built within her and soon the deliberate strokes he maintained were not enough. Rolling, Annie straddled him. His grin mesmerized her as she drove her hips into his. She needed to claim him, leave the kind of mark on his soul that she knew was on hers.

Rafe's hands gripped her thighs, but he didn't attempt to slow her quickening pace. Lifting, he pulled himself into a seated position, growling with pleasure as her ankles locked behind his back.

"Rafe…" Annie twisted her fingers through his hair as she forced their lips together.

His tongue met each of her demanding strokes as she slammed against him. Holding his gaze, she rode him, accepting, demanding all the pleasure he could give. Panting against his shoulder, she crested with him.

Goose bumps rose along her scorched nerves as Rafe's fingers wandered over her back. Tears pressed against her eyes, but she refused to let them fall. She was not going to spend a minute of her time mourning the future. The present was too precious.

* * *

Rafe was going to keep seeing Annie. He wasn't sure how, but he knew he'd find a way to make it work.

The world intruded on his thoughts as his cell buzzed. Sighing, Rafe picked it up, barely resisting the urge to throw it.

Conference call with Dave and me Tuesday at noon—not negotiable.

His stomach clenched as he stared at Carrie's order. His fingers hovered along the buttons.

He still didn't have another interview location to pitch to Dave, and Annie's clinic was amazing. The story of a doctor who managed a thriving miniature ER at the edge of the Arctic Circle would entice anyone. The clinic was remote, exotic and had a gorgeous proprietor who had served her country before turning her sights on an underserved community. Surely it was a story that deserved to be told.

The problem was Charlotte Greene. That was the story Dave and everyone else would want.

His hands shook a little as he typed out the simple word, Fine.

And if Rafe didn't have a better idea by Tuesday… Well, his ratings were still better than the other contenders. That had to count for something.

Show tunes echoed down the hall as he made his way to the kitchen. When Annie came to LA he was taking her to a musical. The thought of Annie in his apartment, visiting his home, made Rafe's heart sing. He would show her his life— find a way to make her part of it.

Annie's voice carried the melody and her wet hair bounced on her back as she swayed.

"Did you ever want to do musical theater?" Rafe slipped his hands around her waist, loving the sigh that escaped her lips.

Pulling the last of the bacon from the pan, Annie turned the oven off before pressing her lips to his. "No. Why?"

Rafe wanted to rub away the tight lines on her forehead. "You're an actress and you love show tunes."

"I'm not an actress anymore." Annie pulled away from him and grabbed a few plates. "I'll get these ready; you pour the coffee."

"Annie…" Her shoulders were tight, but Rafe pressed ahead. If she wasn't running from the past, visiting LA would be easier for her. "Why do you want to pretend Charlotte Greene didn't exist?"

Annie rounded on him. "Excuse me?"

The hairs on his arm stood up, but he didn't back down. "I only asked about musical theater because you love show tunes."

"I am more than Charlotte." Her hands trembled as she backed away from him.

Rafe tried to ignore the shivers running down his back. "Of course you're more than Charlotte. I asked a simple question about show tunes. You can't wipe Charlotte from your slate any more than I can wipe my mother's abandonment or my foster families from mine. She is part of you."

Stepping into her arms, Rafe sighed as she let him pick up her left hand. Annie followed his steps and her breath slowed as she fell into the rhythm of the dance.

It would be better to drop the topic. Let romance spin them around the room. These were the simple moments he craved. It was easy to be romantic with Annie. He wanted to make her smile so he followed the quickest path to see her ruby lips tip up.

"When you come to LA, I bet I can find a theater where they're performing one of these shows."

Rafe managed to keep his face blank as Annie's heel landed on his toes.

"Oh."

She tried to pull back, but Rafe held her tight. He'd meant to *ask* her to come to LA—not make it sound like she'd already agreed.

"I can't come to LA, Rafe. I mean I know it's only a few flights—two if I leave on a Wednesday…"

She'd thought about it and decided against it.

Rafe closed his eyes as pain ripped up his back.

Annie stepped away and he didn't attempt to hold her. "Annie—"

She held up her hand before sliding into her chair. "The clinic needs me."

Heat tore up his neck. She *had* to come to LA—not permanently, but because the city was important to him. His successes were there, and he needed her to see it through his eyes—not Charlotte's. Was this really only about the clinic?

Pushing past his fear of rejection, Rafe tried to make his case. "You're allowed to have a life, Annie. To visit your—"

The word *boyfriend* caught on his tongue. They hadn't discussed their relationship and he hated the label. He didn't want to be Annie's boyfriend—he wanted something more.

Refusing to acknowledge the deep need pulling at him, Rafe pressed on. "I can visit Alaska, but there are times I need to be in LA."

Her gray eyes refused to meet his as she traced an ancient groove in the table. "I haven't left the clinic since I founded it. Liam helps out when he's in town. And I'll try to hire another doctor after winter. But if I'm not here…"

He understood the need to protect your patients. Rafe didn't have the same connection to his as Annie to hers, but he still wanted the best for them. But… "You need to take a vacation, Annie, even if it's not to LA." His voice caught. "It would be good for your patients too, if you had a break."

Her left eye twitched as she glared at him. "I don't need a break."

"You're a true general practitioner, Annie. In an era when most GPs are forced to choose family medicine. You deliver babies, stitch wounds, set bones—do all the general illness things. But this small town is growing. The oil company will be bringing at least a few hundred more people here in the next few years."

Reaching for her hand, Rafe ran a finger along her palm. He needed to touch Annie, calm the racing in his mind that screamed he could lose her.

He refused to worry about that now.

Rubbing Annie's cheek, Rafe kissed the tips of her fingers. "If you don't rest occasionally you're going to fail your patients. Maybe not tomorrow, or next month, but at some point this clinic is going to be overwhelmed with an illness or a mass casualty event, and if you're burned out…" Rafe hated making her unhappy, but she needed to hear this.

Her lip twitched, but she didn't meet his gaze. "Mass casualty?" Annie ran a finger over her lip. "I don't think I need to worry too much about gun violence here."

"I wasn't speaking of gun violence—although it's a sad truth that I don't think you can scoff that away, sweetheart." Placing his palms on the table, Rafe laid out his concerns. "There have been two earth tremors while I've been here. Alaska is part of the Ring of Fire. What happens if a major quake hits this area? What happens if there's an avalanche and you have more than two people buried? Or a mudslide in the summer? Or a flood?"

Her hands shook as she laid her coffee mug on the table and shifted in her chair. "Enough."

She was preparing for battle. Part of him hated forcing the issue, but he didn't back down.

"Annie, you're taking a huge risk by working all the time and not taking care of yourself."

"I take time for myself."

"When? After-hours the clinic phone rings in your bedroom; the front doorbell echoes through your whole apartment; you have an alarm by your pillow for all emergencies. You don't even want to consider a vacation or spend the weekend away."

With me.

"You act like I'm the first physician tied to my work." Her cheeks trembled as she drummed her fingers against the table. "*Your* free time is spent shooting a medical television show and courting fans. That is hardly the life I want."

Rafe sucked in a breath as he stepped back. His heart tore at her sharp tone. He knew she didn't like the show, but she'd helped him with a few research projects since she'd found him looking into hot yoga weeks ago. He had thought she respected what he did. Respected his part in the show.

Annie reached for him and cursed herself as he pulled away. What was *wrong* with her? Rafe was talking about the future. She wanted to talk about what happened next. Why was she picking a fight?

LA, though...

"Rafe—I'm sorry."

Rafe nodded, but the gleam in his eye was gone.

"You're right, Annie. My life is wrapped around my California clinic and *Dr. Dave*, but I have other things in my life too. I can still volunteer at an Alaskan clinic and take the occasional vacation. You're hiding here."

He laid the accusation at her feet.

"I'm not." Annie's fingers shook as he raised an eyebrow. Why was he pushing this?

Gripping his coffee mug, Rafe nodded. "Great. I'll buy you a ticket for LA this afternoon. We can order it for six months from now—that way you'll have all winter to hire a new doctor and get ready to come see LA."

She raised an eyebrow and her bitter laugh shot across the table. "I've seen it, Rafe."

They were the wrong words—again. This morning had gone completely wrong.

"You haven't seen it with *me*, Annie. I want to take you to the places I love, not the TV studios." Rafe pushed his hands through his hair.

"Places like the Thai restaurant where I order so often they know my Tuesday, Friday and Sunday orders. The park where I spend Saturdays taking yoga, parkour or any other random free class that's offered. I want to introduce you to my neighbor Martha. She was a pin-up girl, and she loves to tell stories about her glamour days while serving old store-bought biscuits."

Rafe laughed.

"Fair warning: they taste like cardboard—but she loves them. I wash down two with the horrid green tea she's so fond of. I know there are bad memories for you there, but we could make some new ones too."

Annie wanted to do all those things too, but she hadn't been in LA since she was eighteen. She couldn't go back—she just couldn't.

Stepping into his arms, Annie held him tightly. "Rafe, I can't leave. The clinic—"

Lifting her head, she captured his mouth. He didn't pull away, but the kiss felt off. She wanted to scream. She couldn't lose him—she *couldn't*.

As she broke the kiss Rafe stepped back. "It's fine, Annie. I understand. This place matters too much." He ran a finger along her chin. "I get it. It was just a thought." He brushed his lips against her cheek. "Now I need to grab something before our patients get here."

Annie knew she should follow him—but she couldn't get her feet to move.

She'd spent the morning trying to find a way to keep him. If he lived anywhere else... The selfish thought slapped Annie.

He was right—she *was* hiding.

Blake's picture hovered in the corner of Rafe's eye as he stormed past the living room. Halting, he stared at it. Annie had moved to the Arctic for Blake, but she wouldn't visit LA for *him*.

Pressing his hands to his forehead, Rafe wanted to rip the horrid thought from his brain.

He was trying to make her choose between Blue Ash and LA. She'd always choose Blue Ash. She *should* choose Blue Ash.

Staring at the shelf, Rafe sighed. Had he really expected Annie to view his life, his show, as being as important as her clinic?

Except it mattered to him.

Rafe swallowed the bile rising in his throat. He wanted her to choose him, but they'd known each other for only a month. He didn't need to rush this; he could wait and hope.

* * *

Annie tapped her foot as she waited for Rafe's last patient to finish up. He'd managed to avoid her all day. He'd nodded to her once in passing this afternoon, but otherwise Rafe had always seemed to be occupied when she had a few spare minutes.

She'd hurt him and she wanted—needed—to fix it. She wasn't ready to cross the border to LA, but Rafe was right. She deserved a vacation.

"Rafe."

He smiled at her before he said a quick goodbye to Mr. Hamilton.

Annie waved at Mr. Hamilton before pulling Rafe back into the exam room.

"I'm sorry."

Bouncing from foot to foot, Annie pulled at the torn skin along her thumb.

"I know LA is important to you. And I—" Annie wrapped her arms around her waist. She wanted to promise to come, but the words stuck in her throat.

It was just a city.

Rafe kissed the top her head. "I'm sorry too. I shouldn't have pushed so hard."

"Maybe—"

"Dr. A! Dr. Bradstone!" Miranda's call echoed down the hall.

"We're fine, sweetheart—promise."

Rafe gripped her hand as they headed for the door, and Annie wanted to believe him—but how long would he wait for her to overcome her fears?

"Lily Banister fell off her bike." Miranda was out of breath as she rushed toward them. "Her mom has a towel pressed against her face, but she says you can see her chin bone."

Annie sighed. "Okay."

Before she could warn Rafe that Lily was trying when she felt well and a hellion when she was ill, he was rounding the corner. He was already examining Lily's chin by the time she caught up.

"You're going to need stitches." Rafe winked at the child as she glared up at him.

"I don't want stitches. Dinosaurs don't have stitches."

Rafe raised his eyebrows. "Are you sure? I think I've seen dinosaurs with stitches."

Lily's eyes widened as she tried to determine if Rafe was being serious. Pursing her lips, she squinted—before letting out a giant roar.

Before Lily's mother Tina and Annie could

react, Rafe smiled and laughed. "That was an excellent dinosaur roar. You still need stitches, though."

Rafe reached for Lily's hand and Annie's mouth fell open as the child gripped his hand and followed him to the suture room.

In five short years Annie had stitched Lily's cheek, and her arm, and splinted two broken fingers. The young girl insisted she could do all the bicycle tricks her brothers could. Usually she was right. Unfortunately when she was wrong the damage was epic.

Lily hopped on the table when Rafe asked her to, then turned her attention to Annie. "Are you passing out lollipops or good candy at the carnival tonight?"

Tina cringed as her youngest child's bold question tumbled forth. "She doesn't mean that."

"Tommy says they're bad." Lily pouted as her mom glared at her.

Tina rolled her eyes as she sat down next to her daughter.

Annie covered her mouth. If she laughed, Lily would continue to tell the room what her brother thought.

Rafe grinned at Annie before turning his attention to their small patient. "I need to give you a shot before I can stitch you."

Lily glared at the needle. "I don't like shots."

"Me either," Rafe commiserated. "How about we do a dinosaur roar after the shot—to make the pain go away?"

Lily crossed her arms, but she nodded.

Annie laughed when Rafe and Lily roared. Rafe was an excellent doctor, and great with children. He'd make a brilliant father.

Annie's brain shifted as that thought rolled around her skull. Since Blake had passed, Annie had walled off the desire to be a parent. Rafe had broken down more walls than she'd realized. Of course, if she didn't ever leave Blue Ash, she'd never find out if that dream was possible.

Annie sat at the head of the table and put her hands on either side of Lily's head. "You can show all your friends your stitches at the carnival tonight. I bet they'll look great with your costume."

Lily stuck her lip out. "I'm going as a *fairy*. I wanted to be a man-eating dinosaur."

Rafe slid beside Lily. "I think a fairy is an excellent costume. I'm going to start now, so I need you to stay still."

"Can I get a sticker?"

Annie bit her lip. Lily might be calmer for Rafe than she was with her, but she was still laser-focused on the sticker drawer.

"Stay still and I will let you pick three stickers."

Lily's eyes widened and she gripped the side of the table.

Three stickers? Annie doubted anything would make the child move now.

Rafe talked about dinosaurs, fairies and his superhero costume as he pulled the wound on Lily's chin closed. Lily soaked up each of his words, never budging.

His easy tone sent an aching need through Annie. She didn't want to go to LA, but if Rafe was there…

"All done."

Rafe's happy tone broke through Annie's mental ramblings.

"What's *your* costume?" Lily stuck her tongue through the empty space for her front tooth as she peered into the sticker drawer.

Annie knew Lily didn't really care, but she popped down beside the little girl. She'd been treating Lily since she was three months old.

"Dr. A is going as a candy witch," Tina replied, before Annie had a chance to offer an answer.

"Actually, I was thinking of changing my costume this year."

Tina's mouth fell open before she covered it with her hand. "That's great, Dr. A."

She glanced at Rafe; his eyebrow was raised, but he didn't comment. She'd bought the costume as a surprise for him, but what would he think now?

Annie swallowed the bulge in her throat.

Lily pulled the back of her heart sticker off and stuck it to her nose. "Can fairies eat people?"

Rafe crouched so he could meet Lily's gaze. "I don't think so. Want to do one more roar?"

The room echoed with Rafe and Lily's dinosaur noises and Annie thought her heart might burst. He was a natural with children.

She opened the exam room door. "I need to see to a few things in the office. Dr. Bradstone will walk you to the front."

Lily ignored her, but her mother turned and waved. "I can't wait to see the new costume."

"New costume?" a deep voice boomed across the hallway. "Are you feeling okay, Annie?"

The air in the hall was hot as Annie tried to breathe normally. *Why* had she admitted to having a new costume? She'd ordered it on a whim two weeks ago. She'd tried it on once and put it back in the bag. She'd meant to return it but hadn't been able to. It was new, and different, and she had kept it because Rafe would love it.

Now she just had to have the courage to wear it.

Annie folded her arms. "I *might* have something different. I think I need to get some new candy too."

Liam Henkle's head snapped back. "Did someone finally tell you those sugar-free suckers are gross?"

Rolling her eyes, Annie glared at her partner. "You know, this is information *you* could have passed along."

Crossing his arms, Liam looked at his feet. "You were ridiculously proud of those things— I didn't want to hurt your feelings."

Liam's dark hair was longer than Blake's, but the motion reminded her of his brother. Blake wouldn't have told her the candies were bad either. He'd have dutifully eaten a few to spare her feelings.

Would Rafe have eaten them? No. He'd have said they were terrible and suggested another option. Even if she didn't want to hear it. That was what he'd done this morning—pointed out what she needed to hear—and she'd let him walk away. Let him think he wasn't enough to pull her to LA.

The carnival didn't matter right now. Rafe wanted her to visit his home, and she wanted to try.

Liam was here, so they needed to discuss options for the clinic to make that happen. Fear and excitement warred within her belly, but Annie motioned for Liam to follow her. She was *not* running away from Rafe.

"I need to talk to you," she said.

Liam closed the office door. "Is this about the handsome replacement doctor you're dating?"

"Nothing is a secret in this town," Annie muttered as she closed the office door. "No, this is not about Rafe. Well, not directly."

"Is it supposed to be a secret?"

"No." Annie's fingers ran along her thumb as she stared at the man who looked so much like his brother it had hurt to see him right after Blake's death. Those feelings were softer now. "I don't want to hurt you…or your parents."

"Annie." Liam wrapped strong arms around her. "Blake would have wanted you to be happy. *We* want you to be happy."

Happiness burst like a dam inside her. "I'm glad—because I think we need to put more focus into finding a reliable partner. I want—I want someone we trust in case we both aren't here."

Liam raised a brow as he blew out a breath. "Thinking of heading south?"

Annie shrugged. "I haven't had a vacation for a while."

"Planning a trip to California?" Liam slid into the chair across from the room's lone desk.

"Maybe…"

Annie's knees shook as she tapped her foot. She wanted to see Rafe's home, meet his neighbor and see his life. See if their connection could manage more than a few blissful weeks.

She pulled out a notepad. "I haven't left since we opened—but it's more than that. The town's population is expanding. With the new oil pipeline opening, I expect it to nearly double in the next five years. As it is, the clinic runs six days a week. If we position ourselves right, we could support three full-time physicians and a physician's assistant."

"You don't have to sell it to me, Annie. I've actually been thinking that it's time for me to spend more time in Blue Ash. I should be around more."

"Really?"

Annie leaned forward. Liam had graduated

from med school a few years before her, but he'd never stayed at the clinic for more than six weeks. It reminded him too much of Blake. Time didn't heal wounds, but it made the pain less raw.

Liam shrugged. "I think it's time I pulled a little more weight here—but there are still a few remote locations I need to visit every few months. I planned to discuss it with you after the carnival tonight." His hand pushed through his hair. "Think Dr. Bradstone might be interested in the Arctic life?"

Annie shook her head. Rafe's life was in LA. The TV show was important to Rafe. He'd earned that promotion on *Dr. Dave*, and she wanted him to succeed.

"Rafe doesn't really like the cold. Besides, his show is based in California."

"We could still offer..."

"He's under contract with *The Dr. Dave Show*. You don't just walk away from that—and this isn't about Rafe."

She cared for Rafe.

The word *love* floated between her eyes and Annie sighed.

She *loved* Rafe. That was why she was so terrified of what the future held. Losing Blake had nearly destroyed her—if it didn't work out with Rafe how would she cope?

Blood pounded in her ears. *Love* meant encouraging Rafe's dreams, even if they were based in a city she loathed.

Liam raised an eyebrow. "We don't have to rush into this. I'll stay through the winter… let you have a bit of downtime." Liam winked. "Take a vacation that might or might not be in California."

"Annie—" Rafe stepped through the office door and stopped. "Sorry. I didn't realize you had company." Holding out his hand, Rafe smiled. "I'm Rafe Bradstone."

Liam stood and gripped Rafe's hand. "Liam Henkle—Annie's partner."

Folds appeared along Rafe's forehead. "Nice to meet you."

"You too. I managed to make it back for the Fall Carnival. It's my parents' favorite time of the year."

"And then you'll head out again?"

Annie saw Rafe's lip twitch as he stared at her partner. His posture was tight.

"Liam's actually planning to spend the winter in Blue Ash," said Annie, and skirted around the desk.

Rafe nodded, but he still didn't meet her gaze. Her heart tore as he kept his distance.

"I'm going to make sure the waiting room is clean."

She was halfway down the hall before she realized the office door was closed. What were they doing?

"Are you really planning to stay through the winter?"

Rafe crossed his arms. Annie had made it clear that Liam never remained in Blue Ash for long. It had infuriated Rafe. Liam *had* to know how much she needed help.

"Yes."

Rafe swallowed. If Liam stayed, a major part of Annie's reason for insisting she had to remain in Blue Ash faded.

He pushed the hope from his mind. She didn't want to be in LA and he was not going to force it. He'd take whatever Annie offered him, for however long she offered it. It just hurt that she didn't want *all* of him.

"Annie deserves a vacation," Liam stated, his eyes holding Rafe's.

"I suggested the same thing this morning. She wasn't happy to hear it."

Liam shrugged. "I think she might be coming around to the idea."

Rafe wanted to ask why Liam thought that, but Liam pressed on.

"Annie's very protective of this place."

"Yes, she feels like she owes it to Blake."

Rafe bit his tongue. His chest burned. He knew Annie's connection to Alaska was stronger than his to LA.

"My brother will always hold a special place in her heart."

"As he should," Rafe agreed.

Annie's love for her former fiancé was part of her. He'd never want to strip that away.

"That doesn't mean it should be used to bind her here."

Liam's eyes widened and his lips split apart. "Wow…" Pulling a hand across his neck, Liam met Rafe's gaze. "That accusation cuts a little close."

Good.

Rafe swallowed the word as he leaned back on his heels. Closing his eyes, he sucked in a deep breath. His argument about the clinic's staffing wasn't any different if Liam took Annie's place. The people of Blue Ash still needed a fully staffed facility. And Annie wouldn't be able to relax if Liam was here alone.

Rafe tried to keep his frustration at bay.

"Annie deserves a full-time partner," he said, and his fingers vibrated as he stared at Liam. He'd left Annie, counted on her to tend to his brother's dream. "I know you've been serving the remote communities, but this clinic shouldn't be staffed by only one doctor—whether it's you or Annie. We've seen patients from eight until six most days since I've been here. That doesn't include the after-hours emergencies that have come in too."

A crease crossed Liam's forehead. "How long have you been here?"

"Four weeks tomorrow."

"You care about this clinic?" Liam circled the desk and picked up a notepad.

"Of course—this clinic cares for the whole community. But if you have an outbreak, one doctor is not going to be enough. Two might not be either, but it's at least a start."

"When I was little, a flu outbreak killed over twenty people here," said Liam. "We didn't have a doctor in the community then. It's why Blake was so intent on coming back here as a physician."

That kind of thing could happen again. Rafe kept that fear buried.

"From everything Annie has told me, he sounds like an amazing person. She's made sure his dream has come true, but you need to help her now."

Liam smiled. "I see why she likes you."

Tapping the pad with his pen, Liam jotted a quick note.

"I mentioned our need for a reliable partner the last three times I've been here, but I didn't push. It was the first thing Annie talked about when I arrived today. I'm not sure what you said, but it worked. Can you do me one more favor?"

"Sure."

Annie had mentioned hiring another physician to Liam? Rafe's heart leapt.

"When she visits you, take her picture by her star on the Hollywood Walk of Fame. I've told her it would look great in the clinic."

Fury rolled through him. If he ever managed to get Annie to his home, the last place he was dragging her was to the Walk of Fame.

Leaning across the desk, Rafe growled, "I'm *not* doing that. She isn't interested in that star, or in anything it stands for."

Liam's cheeks puckered as he smiled. "You're a good man."

"That was a test?"

"Yep." Liam winked. "I don't even know if she *has* a star, but I do know she would never want a picture with it. You aren't the only one interested in protecting her."

Before Rafe could find an answer, Annie opened the door. "We need to get ready for the carnival," she told them. Her eyes flicked from Rafe to Liam. "Everything okay?"

"Yep. I can't wait to see your new costume."

Liam laughed as he ducked past Annie.

CHAPTER EIGHT

"ARE YOU EVER going to exit the bathroom?"

Despite the tight faux leather suit, goose bumps erupted across Annie's skin. "Just one more minute."

This wasn't a trip to LA, but she hoped Rafe liked it. Drawing a dark line across her eyelids, Annie took a deep breath. It was now or never.

"I'm coming out. Close your eyes." Annie giggled as Rafe's sigh echoed through the door. "Sorry. That was overly dramatic."

"I've been waiting for this reveal for the better part of five hours," Rafe said, his eyes pinched closed.

"So much drama! It's only been an hour and a half. I just need to put my utility belt on and then the costume is complete."

"Utility belt? I'm intrigued."

Annie took a deep breath. Her cheeks were *not* going to be beet-red when Rafe opened his eyes.

Snapping the belt into place, Annie let her

eyes wander over Rafe's impressive body. He didn't need any help filling out the impressive red, white and blue superhero outfit. He looked like he'd stepped directly out of a comic book.

Rafe folded his arms. "I'm counting to five, Annie, and then I am opening my eyes."

"Go ahead."

She stood up straight and waited. It had taken her over an hour, but she'd managed to straighten her red curls and to cover her freckles with more foundation than she'd worn in fifteen years. If she was dressed in a cotton sun dress with a big bow she'd look just like Charlotte Greene. Instead she was squeezed into a form-fitting costume to match Rafe's.

Annie's arms twitched as Rafe's gaze wandered across her. She was *not* going to fold them across her belly. Did she look enough like a kick-ass spy?

"For goodness' sakes, say something."

"You got a costume to match mine." His Adam's apple bobbed as he stepped toward her. "Not to mention you're dressed in skin-tight leather—"

"*Faux* leather," Annie countered.

"Faux leather..." Rafe muttered as his lips skimmed the base of her neck. "I think my brain forgot how to make words for a second there. You are the sexiest woman I've ever seen."

She loved making him speechless, but worry crept across her belly. "It's a bit different from my candy witch costume…"

Rafe's fingers tripped along her waist and he leaned into her hair. "You look amazing, Annie—but if you would feel more comfortable going in your candy witch outfit, go change."

He kissed her cheek before heading to her closet. The black dress looked shapeless as he draped it across his arms.

"Tonight is supposed to be fun. If you're my partner it doesn't matter whether I'm with the sexiest spy or the wickedly hot candy witch."

Rafe laid the dress on her bed and grabbed her bent witch's hat. It had spent a year stuffed under her sweaters and looked terrible.

Rafe really meant it. He didn't care if she wore the outfit that matched his or went with the safe choice. Her worry popped. Rafe was smiling and the uncertainty she'd felt since this morning vanished. She looked amazing, and she wasn't going to let fear drive her tonight.

Grabbing her water gun, Annie smirked as she placed it in the utility belt. "I think I make a pretty convincing superhero!"

His lips captured hers. The world exploded as his fingers traveled across her back.

Home.

It was a ridiculous word to attach to a kiss.

But as Annie melted against him she sighed. Rafe *was* home. She didn't know what that meant for the future, but she knew she couldn't give him up just because their lives were geographically separated.

Annie's head was leaning against his shoulder. Standing in the crowd around the dance floor, they looked like half a dozen other couples. Maybe this was what love looked like? Rafe sighed. Maybe it really was things like dancing in matching costumes to win a silly trophy that made life rotate from good to amazing.

Rafe didn't know how he was going to keep his LA life separate from Blue Ash, but he was going to find a way. Any woman who was willing to dress as a superhero to match him was worth the world. He'd fly back as often as he could, and maybe they could meet in Seattle every few weeks. Some time with Annie would be better than none.

As a couple and their two children bent and pulled at imaginary cords he cheered with the rest of Blue Ash. The family's rendition of the lawn mower dance was followed by the children bouncing on the floor in an excellent version of the worm, while their parents twisted their hips.

Tapping his own hip against Annie's, Rafe laughed. "I think our swing dance is going to be out of place."

Annie's cheeks burned as she moved her head on his shoulder. "I'm sorry. I meant to tell you a dozen times that our practices weren't necessary. Most of the community probably started practicing only a few days ago—or this morning. I just wanted the excuse to step into your arms."

Rafe didn't know it was possible to be this happy. He pressed his lips against her forehead. "You can step into my arms anytime, my love."

The endearment had slipped out and Rafe tightened his hug, trying to gather his own thoughts. All of them screamed the same thing. He loved Annie; this wasn't a passing chemical high.

The Fall Carnival wasn't the place for a huge declaration, though. She might not think romance needed giant gestures, but he was going to find a special way to tell Annie he loved her.

Shifting topics, to keep from blurting his feelings out in front of the entire community, he nodded to the dancers. "How do we vote?"

Annie studied him, but didn't mention his use of the word *love*. "There are big jars on the back wall. A dollar gets you ten candy corns; five dollars gets you seventy-five. Jar with the most candy corn wins."

"Candy corn?" Rafe glared at the jars. "Why are they using good candy?"

Annie's hand pressed against his chest as she laughed. "Oh, that's *funny*." Her eyes sparkled with the orange lights hanging around the room.

"You don't like candy corn?"

Annie's lips fell open. "It's colored wax. You really like it?"

Rafe shrugged, staring at the jars as they filled up with tiny triangles. "My foster mother Emma used to give us some after dinner. She would have loved everything about this dance." His throat tightened as he remembered Emma's yellow house.

Annie pushed a bit of hair behind his ear. "Tell me about her."

Placing his hands around her waist, Rafe smiled as Emma's tightly wrapped gray bun floated in his memory.

"She swore that bright colors lifted the spirit. I was an angry preteen—I still believed my mother wanted me, and I hated everyone for keeping us apart. I made fun of everything and was generally a horrid brat. I told Emma her bright green-and-pink rooms were ridiculous. I said I preferred black. Made some awful joke about it being the color of my soul."

His cheeks flamed at the memory of his angsty response.

"When I got home from school the next day she'd painted my room black."

He laughed as Emma's cheeky smile floated in his memory. She would have loved Annie too.

He kissed the top of Annie's head as she wrapped her arms around his waist. "She'd used white-and-yellow paint to make star patterns. She told me stars shone brightest in the dark, and she believed I was a star. She swore that one day I'd light up the night." He chuckled. "Maybe that's why I love the spotlight so much."

Annie squeezed his hand. "How long did you live with her?"

"Six months. She had a stroke." Rafe's voice faltered. "Before she passed, she told me to remember I was a star."

"So there was someone who believed in you and she sounds amazing."

Annie pulled him away from the dance floor.

She handed over a five, popped a few candy corns in her mouth and then tossed Rafe the bag.

"Thought you didn't like them?" Rafe said, and sighed as the treat melted in his mouth.

"I don't have the same history with them as you do." Annie kissed his cheek. "But they're not as terrible as I remember."

"A ringing endorsement."

Rafe laughed as he dumped a few more in his mouth. Emma had believed in him—trusted that one day he'd shine. But her words had been lost in his mother's warnings that he'd end up a liar and a user like his father. Now, with Annie by his side, it was easy to believe Emma's words and recognize his mother's remarks for what they were—lies.

"I'll buy you some more after we tear up the dance floor."

He grabbed her hand as she pecked his cheek, "Why have you never participated in the dance before? You're an excellent dancer and this whole town either moonwalks to eighties music or flosses to pop."

Wrinkles crossed her forehead as she stared at him.

Charlotte, he thought.

"You didn't want them comparing you to your character?"

She nodded before leaning toward him. "I don't care what anyone thinks when you hold me, though."

Rafe captured her lips, pulling her tight against him. Her hands wrapped around his neck and he lost himself in pleasure. Annie Masters, this wonderful, compassionate, breathtakingly beautiful woman, had chosen him.

"If the doctors can tear themselves apart for their dance..." A few cheers went up around them as the master of ceremonies held out a hand.

Annie smiled as the shouts echoed around them. She was basking in the attention—because she was with *him*. When he ranked his happiest moments he knew they'd all contain Annie, but this would always vie for position as one of the top nights.

Rafe clasped her hand in his and pulled her into the center of the stage. "Let's show them how it's done!"

Her giggle was drowned out as their peppy swing tune echoed through the speakers. The crowd disappeared as Annie's hips twisted away from him. It was just him, Annie and the music. She glowed each time she landed in his arms.

Rafe gripped her hands as they did the rock horse.

Love. The word hung about them as he matched each of her steps.

He didn't fear telling Annie that he loved her—didn't doubt that she'd want him too. For once, someone was going to choose *him*. He wasn't sure what that meant for his life in LA, but Rafe didn't care. He needed Annie more than anything else.

Annie's chest hit his as they bounced together to the rhythm. A whistle echoed through the crowd as he picked her up, swinging her legs to the left and then the right. Laughter rippled around the room as Annie wagged her finger and danced away from him, her hair tumbling across his shoulders. Finally, she rushed toward him, and Rafe caught her as she swung around his hips.

The community center erupted as the song ended and they bowed.

"Well, folks, that is going to be hard to beat! Voting will remain open for the next hour." The master of ceremonies knocked his hand against the mike, and when that failed to grab the crowd's attention he placed it next to the speaker to create feedback.

Annie pressed her head against Rafe's neck as the squeal blasted through the center.

"Dr. A and Dr. Bradstone's performance was amazing—but there are still three more groups to go!"

Rafe pulled Annie to the side of the dance floor and took his phone from his pocket. Kissing Annie's cheek, Rafe snapped a picture.

"What are you doing?"

"Capturing our moment of triumph!"

"Don't celebrate yet. Someone else might get the trophy."

Rafe flipped the phone toward her. "I don't care about the trophy, Annie."

He didn't. All that mattered was how much Annie had enjoyed the dance. They'd moved together as one, and it had felt magical.

"We danced together, in front of everyone, and you loved every minute. This picture cements *that* triumph!"

Rafe's heart exploded as his lips captured hers. The community center, the congratulations, the trophy, the world—all of it vanished as Annie pressed into him.

"We are *great* together."

* * *

Annie ran her fingers across the picture Rafe had taken before she melted into his kiss. She'd loved every second of their dance. And Rafe was right—it didn't matter if the whole town watched or no one at all. She wanted to dance with Rafe forever.

Cameras were flashing everywhere as Annie and Rafe made their way through the crowd.

"Dr. Bradstone!" A young woman bounced in front of them. "Can we get a picture together?"

Rafe smiled and then frowned. "I don't think now..."

"Go on!" Annie patted his chest. "I'll go stuff our jar with more candy corn."

A tingle crossed her spine as Rafe kissed her cheek. "Save some for me."

Women were lining up, each one wanting their thirty seconds with the handsome TV doctor. Arms were wrapped around Rafe's waist, and he smiled for all of them. Rafe loved the attention.

Annie waited for the jealousy she'd experienced weeks ago to form, but it was just excitement that was rocketing through her. Rafe might have pictures taken with his fans, but it was *her* he wanted.

"That's a great costume." Danny, Mac's grand-son, beamed as he stepped up next to her.

"Thank you. How is your grandfather doing?"

"He's good. Around here somewhere—though Grandma made him promise to take it easy." Danny was dressed in the same costume as Rafe, though his costume was padded to fill out the muscles. He rubbed at his neck before lean-ing toward her. "Can I get a picture with you?"

"Why?" Annie bit her lip as the teen stepped back. "Sorry, Danny. I guess I'm just not used to people wanting pictures with me."

That was a lie; she'd spent years pretending to smile for her fans. Rafe made it look easy, but it had drained her. Cameras and first-gener-ation smartphones had captured Annie at din-ner, working out, or just walking on the street. Flashes of light still sent ripples of unease across her skin.

"I don't look as great as Dr. Bradstone, but a picture with you in that costume would make me look more *real*."

Annie squinted at him. Danny's cheeks were bright red. "You want a picture because of my costume?"

Danny's bushy brows twisted as he frowned.

"Uh, yeah, Dr. A. Why else would I want your picture?"

Placing her hands on her hips, Annie laughed. "I have no idea." She tilted her head. "Let's do this."

Grabbing his plastic shield, Danny handed his phone to a friend before kneeling in front of her. He waited for a moment, before sighing. "Dr. A?"

Annie looked down at him. Why wasn't his friend taking the picture?

He cleared his throat. "Can you strike a pose?"

This really *was* about her costume.

"My apologies, Danny!" Annie pulled her water gun out and held it against her chest as she glared at the camera.

Danny hopped up, looked at the phone and beamed. "Perfect!" He showed it to a few friends and then disappeared into the costumed crowd.

Danny's happiness was infectious. Was this how Rafe felt when his fans swooned over their photos with him?

"For someone who claims she isn't a good dancer, you looked like a professional out there." Holly threw her arm around Annie's waist.

"I might have fudged a little, but Rafe is an excellent partner."

Annie glanced over at him. He was posing with a fan who was wearing a giant inflatable T. rex costume. The image was ridiculous—and perfect.

"I bet he's excellent at other things too." Holly giggled as they made their way to the dessert area.

Holly's baked treats were the real stars of the carnival. People talked about them for months and begged for their favorites to make the annual spread. There were orange pastries that turned your teeth red when you bit into them, ghoul sugar cookies and chocolate-raspberry spider webs.

Grabbing a cookie decorated to look like a witch's finger, Annie winked at her friend. "He's quite skilled in *all* areas."

Her cheeks heated and she pursed her lips. Annie rarely discussed personal topics; she was always worried that people, even friends, would sell the information. Now, though, it seemed like another thing she'd let Charlotte steal from her.

Holly rearranged a few trays. "Good. It would be a shame if he was so attractive but poor between the sheets." Holly's dark skin gleamed in the lights as she winked.

"That is quite the innuendo for Minnie Mouse to make." Annie pointed at Holly's ears as her cheeks burned once more.

Suddenly Rafe's strong arms slid around Annie's waist as he nodded to Holly. She felt secure in his embrace. Any part of the future seemed possible when Rafe's heart beat next to hers.

Annie grinned as she handed him a bag of candy corn. "I got these for you."

"For voting or eating?"

"Your choice." Annie laughed as Holly glared at the bag.

"There is a perfectly good dessert table here, Rafe." Holly pointed to her creations. "And now I need to put out the goody bags. Annie, can you help me grab them from the supply room?"

Rafe popped a few candy corns in his mouth and smiled at Holly. "Why are they in the supply room?"

"If I put them in the kitchen they'll disappear. I only make enough for each kid to have one goody bag. No one looks in the supply room."

"That's because it's a disaster zone." Annie chuckled as she poured a few candy corns in her hand and handed them to Rafe. "Once we fetch them you should help pass them out, Rafe."

Rafe dropped a candy in his mouth. "Why me?"

A child dressed as superhero walked past and high-fived Rafe without breaking his stride.

"Because you are a natural with children," said Annie, and pointed at the retreating child.

Rafe's eyes flickered. "No. I'm not." His voice was strained.

A bead of fire licked up Annie's back. She laid a hand against his cheek. "You calmed Lily this afternoon, and every child in this room has spoken to you tonight. You aren't broken, Rafe Bradstone. And I'm going to make you believe that, no matter how long it takes."

"Annie…" An emotion danced behind Rafe's eyes that she couldn't read.

Laying a finger on his lips, she kissed his jaw. "I have to get the goody bags. Then we'll pass them out together."

"Okay," Rafe muttered, but she knew his focus was somewhere else.

Annie squeezed his hand and ran to catch up with Holly. She tried to ignore the pinch of worry creeping along the base of her neck as she helped Holly get the heavy supply room door open. A box in front of the light switch tumbled over, and Annie let out a cry as the edge caught her arm.

"Are you okay?" Holly flipped the light on and grabbed Annie's arm.

A small stream of blood trickled across her wrist, but it was the slice in her costume that angered her. Superheroes were *never* destroyed by boxes.

"You okay?"

"Yes, I suppose," Annie grumbled, before sighing. The blood was already clotting, and a bit of black thread would fix the rest. "Wow, this place is a mess. After the carnival we need to see about cleaning it out."

Holly chuckled as she stepped over a box of Christmas decorations and the head of an Easter bunny. "I think we say that after every event, and yet…" She held her arms out and sighed.

Bending, Annie grabbed the box that had attacked her. At least she could find it a new location. Kicking at another box, Annie forced her way to the back of the long room.

"This is just ridiculous."

Then the room started to sway, and the box dropped from Annie's fingers. She let out a cry as the piled-up boxes started shifting around her.

Screams echoed from the community center as the earth tremor's shakes became more violent.

"Annie!"

The panic in Holly's voice sent a bolt of terror down Annie's spine. She'd lived in this region for years and the tremors had never lasted this long. The stack of boxes beside her tumbled to the ground.

"I'm fine. Stay where you are."

"Annie—" Holly's words were lost as the roof creaked.

A wooden pallet became dislodged from the wall and pain shot through Annie's head. Her knees cracked as they connected with the floor. She didn't have time to raise her hands before the world darkened.

CHAPTER NINE

ANNIE... RAFE'S BRAIN screamed as he pushed toward the crying people at the front of the community center. He needed Annie. But duty came first. Besides, she was probably racing toward the same scene.

Rafe looked at the sea of heads, desperately searching for her bright red hair.

The small boy who'd high-fived him earlier cradled his arm on the raised stage. A cut ran from his elbow to the middle of his arm. It looked painful, but it wasn't very wide or deep.

Squatting beside him, with a woman dressed as a fighter pilot, Rafe touched the boy's arm. "Can I have a look at that?"

The child sniffed a few times before holding out his arm.

Rafe grabbed an unopened bottle of water and washed off the blood.

The boy pulled away, and Rafe offered him a smile. "What's your name?"

"Mitchel."

"Well, Mitchel…" Rafe tapped his knee, forcing his mind to focus on the kid. "I know you're scared, but I need to check your arm."

The cut wasn't too bad, and he didn't think the little guy needed any stitches.

"You're obviously a superhero, Mitchel, because this will be fine in a few days."

Mitchel's face lit up.

Maybe Annie was right. Rafe had never considered children before, but the idea didn't make him want to flee. That couldn't happen if he was in LA and she was in Blue Ash. Could he give up *Dr. Dave*?

Yes—for Annie he could do anything.

Rafe stood and let his eyes wander across the room. His stomach clenched as he failed to locate her. The room contained most of the population of Blue Ash, but he should still be able to find her. Where *was* she?

Liam rushed to his side. "Mr. McHenry sprained his ankle when he fell after his wife grabbed him, and I think Margery Stevens needs a butterfly bandage for the cut above her eye. Other than that…" Liam ruffled Mitchel's hair. "We seem to have come through unscathed."

"Have you seen Annie?" Rafe's stomach lurched as more minutes passed without her.

"No." Liam sat back on his heels and frowned, his eyes wandering over the room. "But she was a combat medic. Maybe she's treating someone I didn't see." Rafe's eyes drifted over each of the costumed inhabitants. Annie's spy costume and Holly's Minnie Mouse costume had stood out all night. Their absence hung in the community center.

A husky Mickey Mouse skidded to a stop in front of them. Holly's husband.

"Liam…" Doug's cheeks were pale and his eyes refused to stay still. "Have you seen Holly? I can't find her."

Rafe's stomach plunged. "Annie and Holly were going to the supply closet. Maybe—"

Liam's face blanched. He and Doug took off and Rafe's feet pounded behind them. It was only a supply closet. Why were they so worried?

Doug pushed at the door, but it refused to move. "Holly!" Holly's husband pounded against the door, tears streaming down his face. "Liam, I can't get it to move!"

"Let me try." Liam patted Doug's arm.

Several spectators had gathered around, trying to see what was happening. Rafe stepped up to the door, throwing his shoulder into it too. The door finally gave way under the pressure. A Christmas tree scraped across Rafe's arm as it tumbled out of the messy room.

"Dad!" Liam grabbed Jack Henkle by the collar. "Annie and Holly are somewhere in here. We need your help in carefully clearing the boxes and I need Mom to run to the clinic. We need Annie's portable med kit." He offered Rafe a tight smile. "We'll need it for the butterfly Band-Aids at least."

The words provided Rafe with no comfort. Annie and Holly were under this debris and they were quiet.

She had to be fine.

He had so many things that needed to be said.

Sucking in a deep breath, Rafe slid the first box to the side of the door and stepped over three more.

"Annie! Holly!"

Blood pounded in his ears. The shelves on both walls had come loose. He shifted a few more boxes and started passing them to Liam and Doug.

"Holly!" Doug's broken voice poured out behind Rafe.

"Doug!" Holly's voice was pinched as it came

from the back of the room. "I'm behind the shelf on the left side—where we store the Easter crafts."

Doug's elbow shot into Rafe's stomach as he climbed over boxes toward his wife.

"Annie!" Rafe called, praying she'd answer him.

"She's on the other side, Rafe. She—"

The tremble in Holly's voice tore through him.

Annie was fine; she had to be fine. He needed her. Life without Annie wasn't an option.

"She hasn't answered me…"

Liam darted toward Holly as Rafe headed to the other wall.

"Annie!"

The silence was deafening.

"Annie, *please*—"

Rafe's voice broke as he forced his feet to move carefully. The room was a landmine of fallen boxes and chintzy decorations. Annie could be under any of them.

"Annie, sweetheart, please make some noise."

Tears streamed down his face, but he didn't waste time pushing them away. He'd only just found her; he couldn't lose her.

"Annie, *say* something."

Let her be okay. His brain screamed the prayer even as he called out.

"Annie!"

The world without Annie—

Rafe pushed the fear away.

"Annie!"

"Rafe…"

The hushed word was so low Rafe thought he'd imagined it. "Annie—where are you?"

His heart screamed as a box shifted a few feet ahead of him.

"Annie!"

An old wooden pallet lay next to her; her blood was spilled across the top of it.

Rafe dumped a few more boxes. He didn't care where anything landed, provided it was away from her. Pushing at a box marked "Parade Supplies," Rafe stepped over some tinsel and a tipped-up popcorn machine.

He fell to his knees beside her. He'd never wanted to pull her into his arms more, but that wasn't an option. Relying on all his med school training, Rafe tried to examine Annie as if she were any other patient. He couldn't risk hurting her because he was unfocused.

Blood drizzled from a cut above her eye. Her

bangs were matted, but the wound was already clotting.

"What hurts?"

"My head…" Her words were slurred. "I need to sit up."

"No," Rafe commanded. He'd seen this before. After a head injury people were confused, and often tried to stand up and move. It was a defense mechanism—the body's attempt to flee the threat. Unfortunately, it could injure a patient further.

"My head hurts." Annie pushed at his shoulder, scowling.

"Sweetheart, I need you to stay still. You have a concussion, and I need to see if there's any other damage before we move you." Rafe placed a light kiss against the uninjured side of her head before he moved down her body.

"My head hurts!" Annie repeated her complaint, tapping on the pallet. "This fell on me. My brain feels fuzzy."

"I know, sweetheart, but I need to examine you."

Rafe's chest seized as he pressed his finger to the bruise forming on her cheek. The best thing he could do was see to her injuries, but the initial rush of adrenaline had leaked from his body.

He took a deep breath, letting his eyes scan Annie. He frowned and his fingers trembled, but he carefully kneaded the soft skin around her ribs.

She let out a low giggle and groaned. "Don't tickle me!"

Her flailing hand landed on his cheek and pain erupted across his face. His tongue revolted as a coppery taste coated his mouth. At least her ribs weren't broken.

"Sorry… My body feels heavy." Annie's eyes fluttered.

"I'm fine, but I need you to stay awake, Annie." Rafe tapped her nose, ignoring the glare she sent him.

"I'm tired and my stomach hurts." She sighed. "My brain is fuzzy…"

His stomach knotted as she repeated the "fuzzy brain" comment. Concussions were the result of brain swelling. The more confusion she exhibited, the longer she'd take to recover. At least Liam was here, because the clinic was going to be operating without Dr. A for at least a week.

Sitting back on his heels, Rafe knocked a cotton candy machine over and glared at the pink-and-blue dust covering Annie's legs. What *hadn't* they stored in this room? Rotating her ankles, he gently pressed his fingers across the skin there. She whimpered when he moved her knees, but her pants were too tight for him to do a full exam.

Liam dropped down beside him with Annie's med kit. "What's the damage?"

"She has a concussion that's causing nausea, bruised knees…maybe a cracked cheekbone." Rafe ran a hand through his hair. She was hurt, but she was going to be fine. Rafe kept repeating that to himself, trying to force the final tinge of fear away.

Liam stood, pushing a bit more of the debris away from Annie. At least now there was a clear aisle to walk her out.

"Doug's going to bring Holly to the clinic too. Her wrist may be broken."

Sliding his arms around her waist, Rafe gently lifted Annie in his arms.

"I want to go home." Annie leaned her head against Rafe's shoulder.

"Liam?" Rafe nodded toward the door. "Any chance you can get them to cut the lights and tell everyone to let us pass without any fuss?"

"No." Tears slipped down Annie's cheeks as her eyes shifted from Rafe to Liam. "I'm not a diva."

Pressing his lips to her head, Rafe ran his finger along an unbruised section of her chin. "This isn't about being a diva, Annie. We need to take care of you."

Rafe turned, but Liam had already disappeared through the door.

"I could walk…"

Annie squeezed at his shoulder as he carefully walked the narrow path Liam had charted for them. He was not going to ask her to loosen her grip. With her concussion, she was not steady enough to navigate the supply room.

"Let me carry you," he said. "It makes me feel better." It wasn't a lie. Rafe needed her in his arms. His heart needed the reassurance that she was going to be okay.

"I don't like this…" Annie muttered as he maneuvered them through the supply room.

"I know, sweetheart. If you *did* like the feel of a bruised brain I'd be worried."

The room was dark and somber as they made their way to the door.

"I can't believe they stopped the carnival for me."

"Everyone loves you."

Love—the word hung on the edge of his lips. If he'd had any doubts about the emotion, tonight's disaster had cemented his feelings. He loved Annie. She gave him life and breath. And as soon as her head was better he was going to tell her. He didn't know how, but it was going to be a moment she'd always remember.

"We forgot our coats. My mother always got me the prettiest coats…"

"I'm sure someone has noticed me carrying you into the snow without them. I bet they're delivered before we even get the truck started."

Annie's concussion must be muddling her mind if she was bringing up a happy memory tied to Carrie. *Carrie.* How could Rafe tell Annie he loved her when he still hadn't told her about her mother—or that Dave wanted to interview her?

His heart clenched—he couldn't.

"Rafe, my side is going to have a permanent imprint of your fingers."

Swallowing the lump in his throat, Rafe forced himself to relax. "Sorry." He stood her carefully by the truck as he juggled the keys in his hand.

"I can buckle myself," she said, when she got in. But the blood rushed from her face as she turned to grab the buckle. Biting her lip, she gripped the seat belt and jammed it into the clasp. "See."

His nose twitched, but Rafe didn't argue.

"Rafe! Annie!" Helen Henkle rushed toward the car.

"See—coats." Rafe turned to accept the heavy bundles from Helen before draping both coats across Annie's lap.

"Jack will drop the trophy off tomorrow." Helen gripped Rafe's shoulders. "Take care of her."

"Of course."

Before he stepped from her grasp, Helen kissed his cheek. "You're a good man."

"Thank you."

Helen didn't know those simple words held power, and Rafe swallowed the knot in his throat.

Turning, Helen fussed over Annie while Rafe got the truck started. She tried to shut the door softly, but the heavy door's clang still made Annie flinch.

"We won the trophy," he told her.

Annie gripped his hand. "I bet it's the sympathy vote."

"Maybe." Rafe's lips brushed her fingers as heat started to pour from the truck's vents. "Now, I am going to drive slowly. Try to keep your head as still as possible."

"This is *not* how I planned to spend the night."

Annie ran her fingers across her cheek, pressing them against her temple, and then yawned.

Keeping his eyes on the dark road, Rafe chuckled. "I think most of the night went well."

"Sure…" Annie sighed. "I'm tired…" Her voice was groggy and her eyes fluttered shut.

"What *were* your plans?" Rafe raised his voice.

His heart hammered as he let his eyes drift from the road to Annie for a moment. He wanted to shout that he loved her or whisper it softly. Instead, he ran a finger along her uninjured cheek. He understood his need to touch her, to prove to his mind she was safe, but his heart refused to stop pounding.

Rafe tried to focus on keeping her awake. "How *did* you plan to spend the night, sweetheart?"

"I love when you call me sweetheart." Annie laid her hand on his leg. "I just love *you*."

The air in the truck's cab evaporated. Did she mean that or was it the concussion?

"Annie—"

The truck quivered as the right-hand wheel popped into a large pothole. Annie cried out and Rafe cursed. He'd hurt her. Her brain was bruised and he'd lost focus.

His lip trembled and he gripped her knee. "I'm

sorry, Annie. We're almost home." Rafe stroked her leg, trying to calm the shake in his fingers. "I'll take care of you. I promise."

Her fingers covered her eyes. "I know you will. I trust you."

Trust. That word was like a slap in the face. He was hiding too many things. But he could fix that. He *had* to.

CHAPTER TEN

ANNIE STARED AT RAFE, trying to pretend his glassy expression and quietness this morning were symptoms of exhaustion. Over the last three days he'd only left her side to treat a handful of patients. Still, something wasn't right. Her brain fog was finally clearing, but worry pressed against her heart.

If Rafe was awake, his head was buried in his small journal and furiously writing notes. The journal had sat by the bed for weeks. Rafe always jotted down a short note in it before sleep, but it hadn't left his nightstand since he'd done that research on hot yoga.

Now it was his constant companion.

She'd asked about it twice and he'd said he was making a list. She hadn't had the nerve to ask what kind. Was he preparing to leave and trying to put distance between them? Was it because she hadn't agreed to go to LA?

"Damn it." Rafe's brows crossed as he seemed to slash items off today's list.

"I'm worried about you," she said. *And terrified you want to leave me.*

Annie left that fear unstated as she poured more coffee into her mug before taking the seat next to him.

Rafe's lips were warm as they pressed against her nose. "I'm the one who should be doing all the worrying. How's your head?"

"Sore—and my cheek is an ugly purple. At least it matches my knees."

Annie tried to catch his mouth, but her lips met his cheek instead. His avoidance of her kisses sent alarm bells ringing across her mind. *What was going on?*

"Bruises always look worse a few days after the injury. I bet the edges will be lighter tomorrow." Rafe scribbled another note before ripping the page from his notebook.

"Want me to throw that away?"

Rafe stuffed the page into his pocket. "No need. I might decide I need it later. I've done that a few times. I have several torn pages hiding in this journal." He caught his lip between his teeth as he tapped his pen on the table.

It was a reasonable statement. Annie had a

hard time throwing away any notes she took too. But that knowledge did nothing to quiet the fear that he was hiding something from her.

"I didn't know you wrote in your journal so often."

Rafe's brows crossed as he looked up. "I don't. Not usually. However, when I'm trying to solve problems it helps me to make lists."

Problems?

She pulled his free hand into her lap. "What are you working on? Maybe I can help."

"Nothing." His fingers rubbed her palm, but his eyes met hers for less than a second before turning back to the journal.

Annie sighed. Why wouldn't he look at her? Was it her bruises? She'd never considered herself vain, but this morning she'd cried as she pulled her hair into a loose topknot. Purple stains traveled across her high cheekbones, meeting in a jagged cut at her temple.

She didn't look like a pretty actress right now. Was that why Rafe couldn't look at her for more than a few seconds?

Drumming her fingernails against her coffee mug, Annie tried to push the worry away. Rafe wasn't a shallow man, and the bruises would fade. Of course his kisses would be more reserved because she was suffering from a concussion. These suspicions didn't serve either of them.

Still, she couldn't shake the uncertainty clawing across her spine.

There were other reasons he might be pulling away.

Was he upset that she'd told him she loved him? *Had* she told him? Her memories were cloudy apparitions, shrouded in pain. She was almost certain her feelings had slipped out through her fog of confusion.

She remembered Rafe calling her his love before their dance, but a term of endearment wasn't a declaration. Annie had combed her muddled memories, but she was certain he hadn't said he loved her. She knew her brain, even bruised, would have retained *that* memory.

Fear had seemed to be her constant companion since the carnival. She wanted to talk about their future, offer to go to LA for a few days, but Rafe was too concerned with whatever was in that journal.

Annie didn't know how to go back to the happy bubble they'd lived in before her injury. Her heart pounded as tears filled her eyes. She didn't want to spend the rest of his time here pretending she was okay with this shift.

"Did I do something wrong?"

The words had escaped. There was no way for Annie to draw them back, and she didn't want to. She needed an answer—even if it ripped her heart in two.

"What?" Rafe's mouth hung open as he stared at her.

Dipping her head, Annie shrugged. "You've been…" Annie hesitated, not wanting to accuse him of anything. "Distant. You're always taking notes and…" The last of her courage evaporated. "Maybe I'm just being nosy, and it's certainly not my place…"

The rambling words echoed in her head. At least she could blame the concussion for her circular thoughts.

Offering a soft chuckle, Annie started to stand, but Rafe grabbed her hand.

"You haven't done anything wrong." His eyes wandered across her bruised features and his fingers squeezed hers. "I just…"

She held her breath as he paused. Why couldn't she push away the fear that he was hiding something?

"I have a meeting with Dave and my agent at

noon. I keep trying to find the answer to a question they have, and my mind refuses to give it." Rafe let out a bitter laugh. "I swear my brain is stuck on repeat."

"No fair—that's *my* excuse." Annie kissed his lips. Her aches disappeared as Rafe deepened the kiss and pulled her into his lap.

"If you weren't black and blue…" Rafe leaned back in the chair. His smile was wide, but it didn't quite reach his eyes.

"What's their question?" Annie leaned her head against his chest. She always overthought things—maybe this question really was all that was weighing on Rafe's mind. "My TV show experience is dated, but I remember the nerves."

Meeting with producers and directors had always left her stomach in knots. And sharing her home with her agent had meant any notes she'd been given had been drilled into her at the dinner table, before bed and first thing every morning. Just the memories sent a shudder through her.

"Dave wants me to do an interview. Actually, I *have* to do the interview."

Annie frowned. "You talked him out of the hot yoga topic. I'm sure you can talk him out of this."

Rafe kissed her forehead. "I've tried. He seems set on this one. He even responded to my last email by forwarding a copy of my contract. If I don't provide something I'll be in breach, and the penalty is steep. It will wipe out all my savings, plus some."

His breath hitched and his arms tightened on her waist.

"I need something to wow him—something he can't say no to."

Annie's heart pounded and she closed her eyes to keep the tears at bay. If this interview went well his contract wouldn't matter. They'd negotiate a new one with his promotion. Rafe hadn't said those words, but she knew how Hollywood worked. He might not like Dave's interview topic, but the show was his dream. It was what mattered to him most.

"What's the topic?"

Rafe's eyes were hooded, and Annie felt the pinch of fear again.

"Rafe?"

Rubbing his hand along his neck, Rafe looked at her. "He wants me to do something that doesn't have any real medical focus. But I've never done gimmicks. I don't want to start now."

Annie had dealt with the fallout of Dr. Dave's fad diets and vitamin gimmicks in several of her patients. It was good that Rafe was telling

Dave no. So why did it feel like there was more to the story?

Rolling her head slowly, Annie forced the uncertainties away. Rafe hadn't given her any reason to doubt him. This was just her fear about the future transferring itself to everything else. After his meeting was over she and Rafe were going to talk—and she was not going to chicken out.

She focused on the thing weighing against his mind. "We don't have much time. Let's get brainstorming. What other ideas do you have?"

This was important to Rafe, so it had to matter to her. Their relationship could weather the long distance and his fame—she had to believe that.

Rafe's arms fell from her sides. "You don't mind helping me with my *Dr. Dave* material?"

Sitting back, Annie pulled on all her acting skills. She needed to look happy for him. "You want that promotion, Rafe. And it should be yours."

"I didn't mention the promotion." Rafe's arms trembled as they wrapped around her again. "And you don't watch *The Dr. Dave Show.* So why do you think it should be mine?"

"You've talked about that promotion since you arrived. It's not hard to read between the lines— even with a bruised brain. You want them to choose you…to recognize what you bring to the table."

Rafe bit his lip. "It's always nice to be chosen."

For a moment Annie didn't think they were talking about the show. But she swallowed and forced that hope aside.

Tapping his cheek, Annie kissed his nose. "I don't watch the show, but I'm biased as hell about the wonderful Dr. Bradstone."

Annie loved the smile beaming on Rafe's features. Hopping off his lap, she sucked in a breath as the world tilted around her.

Rafe caught her before she could topple over. "You still need to move slow, sweetheart."

"I love that you call me that…" The words slipped into the quiet kitchen.

Rafe kissed the top of her head before helping her back to the chair. "Well, I *like* calling you sweetheart."

She'd never had a nickname. Most people assumed her real name was Anne, but her mother had chosen Annie because she'd thought it sounded like a good stage name. Annie rubbed her finger on the rough skin of her thumb. Even as a child, her mother saw her as a potential subject to turn famous.

When *she* had children, she'd make sure

they had cute nicknames for Rafe to whisper in their ears.

Chills warred with warmth as Annie stared at Rafe. And as the image of him chasing dark-haired children soaked through her she sighed. He'd be an excellent father. But that life couldn't exist if they were thousands of miles apart.

Could she leave the clinic?

That question had seemed impossible even a week ago. There were plenty of practices in LA, but Blue Ash had meant everything to Blake. It meant so much to her too. But if she wanted a life with Rafe she had to find a way to live in the same state as him. If he needed the spotlight, she would find a way to stand beside him.

"Come on—tell me your ideas." Annie gripped his hands. Relationships were partnerships; she could do this—for *him*.

Rafe clicked his tongue and picked up his journal. "How about we brainstorm while snuggling on the couch? You can help me weed out all the awful ideas."

"I bet you have at least one winning idea in there."

He was so talented; she knew Rafe was destined to sit in one of the permanent chairs on Dave's set.

Annie ran her hands along the wall of the hall. She knew where each dip and hole of the clinic's log cabin walls was—but this hadn't always been home. Home was where the people you loved were. It was with Rafe.

"I don't know why you keep trying to add more topics. Discussing the lack of medical support in rural and low-income communities is the best."

Annie crossed off all the other topics they'd hashed out over the last hour.

She was right—but Rafe didn't want her to think he was looking to interview *her*. Rafe knew how much she hated the spotlight. She'd been exploited by her mother and the Hollywood machine. He didn't want to perpetuate that for his own gain—wouldn't perpetuate it.

"Annie…" Rafe's tongue stuck to the roof of his mouth. "If I do this, what should I highlight?"

Her eyes narrowed. Did she think he was using her? Nothing could be further from the truth. Rafe had spent every day trying to find another topic for Dave. He'd scoured his contract, but Dave was within his rights to demand a specific topic.

However, if Annie didn't agree to the interview Dave couldn't force *her* to participate. But Rafe hadn't asked her. Annie was kind, compassionate and supportive. She might agree to it to help him get the promotion. Except that the promotion didn't matter much when she was beside him.

Rafe had to find another avenue without risking her.

"I remember seeing an infographic from the American Medical Association a few months ago. I think the greatest shortages are in Mississippi and Idaho. It isn't just locations, though..." Annie pushed a curl behind her ear.

Rafe ran his fingers along the top of her thigh. It was one of the few places where she wasn't bruised. His need to touch her had only increased since her accident. He'd woken from the same nightmare every night since the carnival. He kept running down crowded aisles in a storage room, but he could never reach Annie.

He couldn't risk losing her—nothing was worth that.

After this meeting he'd wrap the final threads of his life together. Then he was going to tell her everything. Buy a huge box of donuts and declare his love. He'd planned his gesture over the last three days. It was going to be perfect.

Rafe forced himself to focus. "What do you mean, it isn't just locations?"

Annie started to shake her head, but caught herself. Her concussion was healing faster than he'd expected, but he knew she was still frustrated with the limited range of motion her brain allowed.

"If the AMA's predictions are correct, we're going to be desperately low on general practitioners, psychiatrists and OBGYNs in the next two decades."

"Hmm… I might have the perfect interviewee for that." His phone buzzed and his stomach rumbled. "But I need to grab a sandwich and place a quick call before the meeting."

"No." Annie kissed his cheek. "I'll make lunch. You head into the bedroom and make that call." She glared at his phone. "Maybe after this meeting your phone will stop buzzing all the time!"

Rafe laughed. "That was *your* phone, sweetheart."

Joining his chuckles, Annie checked her phone. His stomach lurched as she frowned. Was something wrong?

"Annie?"

"Jenn's dad has to have emergency heart surgery. Guess it's a good thing Liam is planning to hang around this winter."

His replacement wasn't coming, and Liam

would need to spend at least a few more weeks in the remote communities before coming back.

"Annie—"

She patted his knee as she interrupted him. "It's fine, Rafe. This was always a possibility." She forced a smile as Rafe's phone dinged. "That is your life calling. Go make your call and do your interview. You've earned that promotion."

"Annie—"

Her eyes were downcast. She'd asked him if everything was all right this morning. Was she doubting him?

His lungs refused to accept any air. He hadn't said he loved her—hadn't convinced her she was what mattered, not the promotion. She didn't yet realize he'd choose her—always. They'd spent the morning planning his interview with Dave. Now his replacement wasn't coming and there wasn't time—

Rafe's phone buzzed again.

Why didn't life have a pause button? There was so much to say.

I love you.

"We need to talk."

"There isn't time." She kissed his cheek. "I'm rooting for you."

Annie disappeared into the kitchen. He should go after her—his soul cried out for him to follow.

The ding of his phone forced his hand. But as soon as this meeting was over Rafe was turning off his phone and he was going to tell Annie how much he loved her. They'd find a way to make this winter work.

Soon…

CHAPTER ELEVEN

IT WAS TEMPTING to drop a few pieces of ham on a piece of bread and rush a sandwich in to Rafe before his meeting started. Part of her brain still screamed that she should do it, but she refused to give in to the cowardly desire. If Annie planned to be a part of Rafe's life she'd meet Dave and his agent soon anyway.

Pushing her fears away, Annie turned the griddle on. Rafe was right: she was more than Charlotte Greene. It was time to step out of the past—particularly if she planned to spend some time in LA.

Her phone buzzed.

Annie tried to ignore the sadness pushing against her. It wasn't Jenn's fault. Annie would just have to push her vacation to springtime. At least with Liam in town the winter wouldn't be too lonely. Except without Rafe—

Annie pushed that thought aside. She was not going to beg him to stay.

Taking a deep breath, Annie swallowed the dread tingling in the back of her throat. She loved Rafe. She wanted to believe he loved her too. But he'd never said it. He was worried about his contract. She understood that panic. Studios were ruthless. She was just overthinking this.

Again her phone interrupted her mental wanderings.

She tried to understand the words on the screen. Helen never texted her—she claimed it was too difficult for her to see the tiny letters on her phone.

Annie's fingers trembled.

I am so sorry. Let me know if you want Jack to fly him to Anchorage this afternoon.

Helen's message was followed by a link to an online tabloid.

"No!"

The phone tumbled from her fingers—its case shattered as it connected with the kitchen tile. Tears floated in her eyes, but she refused to let them fall. Bending, Annie retrieved the phone. She was tempted to let the story remain unread, but maybe it was false. Tabloids made their money off half-truths, paid informants and lies.

Sucking on her lip, Annie followed the link.

Playboy Doctor Uses Child Star to Secure Promotion

The picture Rafe had snapped after they'd stepped off the dance floor headed the article.

Only he had that image. Only he could have given it to the press.

He'd lied to her…made her believe—what?

Rafe had never said he loved her. He'd said they needed to talk.

God, she was a fool.

When Dr. Rafe Bradstone departed for Alaska a few weeks ago his fans assumed it was an escape—a few weeks away to rehab his playboy image. But apparently the Playboy Doctor wasn't just volunteering his medical expertise. Instead he was seeking a desperate starlet, hiding in the wilderness.

CelebNews Weekly *has learned that Dr. Rafe Bradstone has secured the permanent co-host spot on* The Dr. Dave Show. *How? By scoring an exclusive interview with child star Annie Masters.*

Ms. Masters currently works at a clinic

in Blue Ash, Alaska. The clinic had not responded to our message left on its answering service by the time of reporting.

Dr. Bradstone's agent, Ms. Carrie Forester, refused to comment, citing a formal press release to be issued later. Ms. Forester also refused to comment on Annie Masters. Ms. Forester is, of course, Annie Masters' mother, and was her longtime manager during her daughter's successful decade-long career on My Sister's House.

Has Annie Masters spent all her wealth? Is that why she's working in an outpost clinic in Alaska?

CelebNews Weekly *will update this story as more details are unearthed.*

Bile coated her tongue, and she had to take several deep breaths to settle the nausea rolling through her stomach. The writer hadn't even bothered to research the clinic. The deed was publicly available—as was her medical license. Even her Army enlistment would be easy to find—several magazines had run short pieces about it. It would have been easy to discover she wasn't a desperate or destitute starlet—but that didn't bring website clicks and ad revenue.

Dr. Annie Masters had been reduced to a "child star" and "desperate starlet." She was so much more, but no one had ever seemed to see it.

Rafe had almost made her believe, but that was a lie too. Her transformation from child star to doctor at an outpost clinic was the perfect leverage for his interview—Annie had even given him a picture for the cover.

Now this morning's snuggles were tainted. Rafe had needed a reason to interview *her*. An interview about the need for healthcare professionals in remote areas—how could she have been so blind? He'd even managed to make it seem like it was her idea. Of course he knew "the perfect interviewee"—she'd been sitting next to him.

Her fingers trembled as she finished reading the story. It was all about *Dr. Dave*. Rafe had told her it was the most important thing. Annie had hoped she'd take that spot eventually, but now—

She closed her eyes as pain rolled through her.

If he'd asked, she'd have immediately agreed.

Her chest was tight and black dots floated before her eyes. Why had he had to make her believe he wanted her? Cared for her?

Annie's lungs refused to fill and she sat down on the floor. She couldn't risk reinjuring her head.

Carrie was his agent. *Her mother.* Carrie had managed Annie's childhood and, given the chance, would still be directing her life. Everyone saw Annie as Charlotte Greene because Carrie hadn't allowed Annie to be anything else.

But Army enlistment contracts were binding. Carrie had screamed, but she'd been forced to let Annie go. She hadn't spoken to her daughter since.

Carrie.

Annie leaned her head against the cabinet. Rafe had talked about his agent since his arrival. How had she failed to notice that he'd never used her name?

Her phone buzzed. Holly's name flashed, along with the link and an offer for Doug to haul Rafe out of the clinic.

This was going to be her life for at least the next several days. Answering polite, probing questions about Rafe's lies. She couldn't stay here—couldn't watch the pleasant smiles as people asked how she was, listed Rafe's faults and told her she was better off without him.

Laying her phone aside, she closed her eyes—what was she going to do?

Six new messages popped in and she put her fist in her mouth to keep from screaming. The last thing Annie needed was for Rafe to come running to her aid.

"Annie?" Liam stepped into the kitchen.

"Don't ask any questions about him, please."

She bit the words out, pressing her palm into her forehead. Her head was screaming, her heart was crying, and her bruised brain didn't know how to handle any of it.

"I need you to ask your dad to fly Rafe out tonight. Can you handle it here alone for a week or so? Even if my concussion was healed..." Annie sucked in a breath "...I just can't stand the looks."

"Of course." Liam's keys landed in her lap. "Why don't you stay at my cabin? It's fully stocked. I can use your guest room here."

"Thank you." Her lips trembled, but she held herself together.

"Where is he?" asked Liam.

"In a meeting with my mom and Dave. Bet he's letting them know how he got me to agree to participate in his stupid interview."

She leaned her head against her knees. She should have realized what he was doing.

"You've agreed?"

Pursing her lips, Annie stared down the hall to where Rafe was probably promising her help right now. "No—not really."

"I'll handle that, then." Liam stepped beside her.

Annie sucked air between her teeth as she stood up and pulled Rafe's half-burned grilled cheese from the skillet. His lunch was still edible, but it wouldn't taste good. Did it make her a horrible person that she was happy about that?

"Please don't…" Annie shut her eyes, praying the tears would stay buried. "Please don't be cruel to him. He— He—"

"If you're about to tell me he doesn't deserve it, I will lose it," said Liam.

Annie swallowed the lump pressing against her throat. She loved Rafe—it hurt that she'd misread his actions, but she didn't hate him. Couldn't hate him.

"Rafe is driven and talented. I told him I was rooting for him to get this promotion. I wasn't lying. I hate the way he did it, and that he didn't tell me, but he needs the show. It makes him feel whole."

She'd thought she soothed some of the wounds on his soul… But she couldn't let her mind wander that path.

"He doesn't deserve you."

Annie didn't have any more words. She wanted to get out of the clinic before Rafe's meeting ended, but she refused to play the coward. Her chest seized; she couldn't make a bigger fool of herself…

Annie nodded to Liam as he went to call Jack and then tell Rafe and his companions that their clinic was not available for *The Dr. Dave Show*.

Her phone buzzed, and she turned it off without checking the message.

Walking downstairs to the clinic, Annie played the voicemails on the clinic's line—twenty-nine calls from different tabloids, and even a few news outlets. Charlotte Greene's image had taken over her refuge, and Rafe had invited them in.

Annie let the dreams Rafe had awakened die with each press of the delete button.

Pacing next to Annie's bed, Rafe stared at the number on his phone. Annie was right: this interview *should* be about the need for doctors in underserved areas. And she was a great reference, but she wasn't the only physician serving in the trenches. Rafe's college roommate, Dr. Demarcus Martin, ran a free clinic in one of the poorest counties in Mississippi.

Demarcus didn't approve of Rafe's participation on *The Dr. Dave Show*, but he might be interested in this topic.

"If you're going to call, stop talking to yourself and push the button," he told himself aloud.

Demarcus was unlikely to answer, but he could leave a message. Pushing his hand through his hair, he closed his eyes and listened to the rings.

"Rafe!" Demarcus's warm tone echoed in Annie's room.

"I want to catch up, but I—I don't have a lot of time…" Rafe stuttered.

"This is related to your show?"

"It is," Rafe muttered as he pulled up his notes. "But how you manage to make *show* sound like a curse word is beyond me."

Demarcus huffed. "Doctors should be serving the community—not strutting like peacocks on the small screen."

Rafe flinched at the harsh words. "Ouch!"

Demarcus sighed. "That is mostly directed at Dave. I'm not interested in flying out for an audition."

"This isn't an audition. It's an interview. Just

listen…" Rafe outlined his plan, watching the minutes tick away. "We aren't educating enough physicians to cover the needs of our remote and low-income population."

"I've seen the AMA's predictions," Demarcus growled. "I don't see what that has to do with my clinic."

Tapping his foot, Rafe made sure the camera and microphone were off on his laptop. Dave never called in on time, but if today was an exception Rafe didn't want him overhearing his next statement until Demarcus was on board.

"Your community is dreadfully underserved. This interview would let us talk about your community's current requirements and highlight the need for reform in med school costs, healthcare expenses, and the uneven access to medical care across the country."

The phone was quiet for a few seconds, and Rafe checked twice to make sure the call hadn't been dropped.

"Not sure that makes great television…but it's a piece I can get behind. Sure—count me in."

Rafe punched the air. "*Yes!* You are *not* going to regret this."

Rafe let out the breath he hadn't known he'd been holding. His contract was up at the end of the year. He'd do a quick trip to Mississippi next week, interview Demarcus, then fly to California, film the Thanksgiving and Christmas shows and then put his life in LA behind him. This piece would be his final legacy in Hollywood.

Dave wouldn't like him withdrawing his name from the promotion pool, but Rafe didn't care. He might have kept a few secrets, but he was free to tell them all to Annie now. He might never be as perfect as Blake, but he was going to spend the rest of his life making Annie happy. Helping her fulfill her dreams here.

"Rafe?"

The quiet quality of Demarcus's voice sent a shiver across Rafe's spine.

"I am not sure how you managed to get Dr. Annie Masters to agree to this too, but one day I want to hear that whole story."

"What?" How did Demarcus know about Annie?

His computer screen started to ring.

"I'll call you with the details in a few days. Thanks, Demarcus."

He knew Dave wanted an interview at the Arctic clinic, but he would make him understand that Demarcus's clinic provided a better example. People expected the Arctic to be sparsely populated, but Demarcus served nearly a thousand patients on a shoestring budget. And it was happening in a town that looked more like everyday America.

Rafe slid into the chair, barely managing to click off his phone before Carrie appeared in the center of the screen.

"Congratulations, Rafe!"

Blood rushed through his ears as Carrie raised her water bottle to him. Why was she congratulating him?

"I take it you haven't seen the *CelebNews* site?" She grinned.

"No, why? Did you leak something to the press?" Raising an eyebrow, he tried to calm the worry pressing against his chest.

"Not me..."

Her gray eyes almost matched her daughter's, but they didn't contain Annie's warmth. Rafe wasn't sure he believed her, but a three-way conference call was not the right time to have an argument with his agent.

His belly rumbled and he looked at the door. What was Annie fixing for lunch?

"Rafe!" Dave's cheery tone echoed around Annie's bedroom. "Is that a *bed* in the background?

I expected to see the clinic." Dave folded his arms as he sat back in his chair.

"I'm in the apartment above the clinic. The doctor I'm helping was injured this weekend, so the clinic is only open for emergencies through Thursday. Luckily we haven't had any of those, but if the bell rings I'll need to step away."

Rafe made a show of pulling up his notes. This was a pitch meeting—not a sightseeing tour of Annie's clinic.

"Well, the duvet makes a nice touch." Dave didn't manage to hide his sneer quickly enough.

Rafe wanted to immediately jump to Annie's defense, but he had no plans to bring her into this talk.

Carrie had other ideas. "How *is* Dr. Masters?"

"She's fine."

Carrie nodded at the perfunctory statement, but didn't push for more information. How could she have raised such a caring woman?

Annie was right—genes didn't matter much. His mother had walked away from him, abandoned him, but he was never going to leave Annie. If she was willing to keep him Rafe would make sure she and—if they were lucky—their children always knew how much they were loved.

"Good." Dave leaned into the screen. "Rafe, the interview team will be there next Wednesday."

"Wait." Rafe slapped the desk, feeling it wobbled with the pressure. "I plan to do this interview at a clinic in Ransburg, Mississippi. Dr. Demarcus Martin is prepared to talk about the same issues we would discuss here."

Dave took a large sip of green smoothie. His voice was diplomatic, but unyielding, when he started his argument.

"Mississippi isn't exotic like the Arctic. I'm not bending on this. This is a television show—we don't want people getting bored. Boredom leads to low ratings and cancellations." Dave looked at his nails and frowned. "I've leaked that you're the new co-host, but we can retract that." His eyes narrowed.

New co-host? Rafe's mind swam. He'd focus on that after Dave agreed to let him do the interview at Demarcus's clinic.

"This is an important segment, Dave. We have a responsibility to use our platform."

"We have a responsibility to our network producers. They are the ones who pay our salaries."

Rafe rubbed at his face. "Then make the producers understand. You're a *doctor*!"

His stomach plummeted when Dave shrugged. "Rafe, you understand the math here. Your suggestions always steer the show to higher-rated stories or away from things that might result in lawsuits. You're a brilliant tactician."

Dave didn't care about the message they provided—only the ratings and the ad revenue that message produced. Rafe followed the ratings, but for him the stories, and helping their viewers, came first. Except Dave hadn't seen that. He'd seen a man determined to sit in the spotlight—driven by attention. A man like him.

How could he have been so blind?

Drawing in a deep breath, Rafe tried once more. Even if he never sat on Dave's TV set again, this was a message he needed to get out. And Demarcus was the perfect spokesman. "I really think if you could see Demarcus's clinic you'd understand. The work he's doing is remarkable—"

Dave clicked his tongue as he interrupted. "Is this Dr. Martin a former child actor who disappeared from public life? Is he running a clinic on the edge of the world? Did he serve as an Army medic?"

The air rushed from Rafe's lungs as he tried to

make sense of Dave's words. How did he know about Annie?

"I—"

"Charlotte Greene is the story I want—not her clinic."

"Her name is *Dr.* Annie Masters," Rafe growled.

Dave's eyes widened, but he didn't say anything.

"How did you know about her?"

Rafe's eyes cut to Carrie, but she shook her head. His stomach turned and the eggs he'd fixed for him and Annie this morning threatened to reappear.

"How?"

"Everyone knows about Annie. The clinic's phone is ringing off the hook."

Liam Henkle's cool voice cut through the bedroom as he leaned against the doorjamb.

"Congrats on the promotion."

Liam tipped his head toward Rafe before he marched to the desk.

"My apologies for interrupting. *Dr.* Masters has asked me to speak on behalf of *our* clinic. We are not going to permit you to do any interviews here."

Dave sputtered, but Rafe didn't care. His entire body was frozen. How had Dave learned about Annie and why was the clinic phone ringing so much?

"I'll call you back."

Rafe closed the laptop without waiting for Carrie or Dave to say anything.

"Annie!"

Ignoring Liam, Rafe tore through the apartment. A burned grilled cheese sandwich sat on a plate in the kitchen. Grabbing his coat, he rushed for the clinic.

"This is Richard Dixon from *Gossip Weekly*. We are attempting to reach Annie Masters. My phone number is—"

The voicemail message was cut off and another started in its place.

"This is Josephine Warren from *All Celeb News*—"

Annie's gray eyes met his as she hit the delete button. "Congratulations on your promotion."

Rafe felt as if his soul had been ripped from his body. "How…?"

He didn't realize he'd spoken the word aloud until Annie spun the clinic's laptop around.

Playboy Doctor Uses Child Star to Secure Promotion

The picture he'd taken of them at the carnival was splashed above the headline. It had come from his social media account. Rafe must have uploaded it without thinking. Annie was just Annie to him—didn't she know how much she meant to him?

The answer crushed him.

No.

He'd kept those words locked away. Instead he'd delivered the media to her door. All his plans to keep her safe looked like manipulation. His motivation was different from his father's, but the result was the same—he'd hurt the woman he loved.

"You should have asked before you had it splashed across the front page of *CelebNews*."

Annie had a green duffel bag sitting next to her feet.

"This isn't what it looks like." Rafe shook his head. "Annie, sweetheart..." Blood pounded in his ears—what was he supposed to do? "I didn't mean—"

The phone rang and Annie's jaw clenched, but she picked it up.

"Blue Ash Medical Clinic. No comment."

She slammed the phone down.

"Didn't mean to make it so I have to leave my

own home? Didn't mean for me to find out about the interview? Or didn't mean to hide the fact my mother is your agent?"

Annie caught back a sob as she picked up the bag.

"Didn't mean to make me believe you cared about me? That I was more than Charlotte Greene to you?"

"I *do* care. God, Annie—you are so much more than Charlotte Greene. Why can't you see that?"

A bitter laugh left Annie's lips as she glared at him. "It's what everyone expects me to be. No matter what I do, everyone I love wants Charlotte. My mother needed Charlotte to advance her career, and you—"

Another choked sob echoed from Annie's chest as she rubbed the back of her hand across her nose.

"I even made it easy for you. You can't tell what my Halloween costume is in that picture, but I'm a dead ringer for an older Charlotte Greene."

Annie pointed to the computer, but Rafe refused to look away from her. She loved him, and he'd delivered a nightmare to her haven.

"This isn't what it looks like," Rafe repeated as he pulled at his hair.

"So you *weren't* given a promotion in exchange for getting me to tell Dr. Dave's audience how I went from being Charlotte Greene to Dr. Annie Masters? The worst part is, if you'd asked I would have agreed to it. I would have said yes to help you. I am *such* a fool."

How had he managed to destroy this so completely? It didn't matter that Rafe had been trying to protect Annie. He'd left so many things out—and lies of omission were still lies.

His body shook. "You are not a fool. You are amazing, beautiful—"

"And the key to extending your time in the spotlight." Glaring at the screen, she shuddered. "Is this enough attention for you?"

Rafe flinched as she leveled that barb at him. How had this day turned into such a nightmare? But before she threw him away he needed her to know one thing.

Gripping her hand, Rafe pressed his journal into her fingers. "This wasn't about Charlotte— it's never been about Charlotte for me. Please read that. I want you to see yourself the way I do. See the intelligent, caring, beautiful creature that you are. I want you to look in the mirror and see Annie."

Annie stared at the journal, but she didn't drop it.

"I took that photo because I was happy to be with you."

I love you. The words stuck in his throat. His mother had thrown those words into arguments, trying to make his father stay. Rafe wasn't going to use them that way.

Annie hesitated for a moment and his heart sped up. Then the phone rang. Annie slipped past him as Rafe picked it up.

"No comment!"

A single tear slid down her cheek. "You promised not to use me." She bit her lip as the phone rang again. "I trusted you, and you shone your spotlight *here*. Now I have to leave the place I carved out for myself—the place where I was supposed to be just Dr. A."

He *had* used her. Not to get the promotion, but to put the pieces of his heart back together. He'd used her to find the meaning of love.

"Please don't walk away."

"There's nothing here for me. Goodbye, Dr. Bradstone."

I'm here... Choose me... Believe me...

He wanted to scream, to beg her to stay, but the words stuck in his throat as she headed out the door. Instead Rafe stepped aside. His father had destroyed his mother with his infidelities, and Rafe's need for the spotlight had taken the thing Annie loved most from her—her clinic.

"I love you..." Rafe whispered as the clinic door slammed shut.

CHAPTER TWELVE

"I'LL HELP YOU PACK."

Liam's gruff comment hit Rafe's back as he watched Annie get into her truck.

"No."

The word surprised Rafe as it slipped from his lips. It felt right, though. His father had run away from his marriage. His mother had run from her parental duties. Rafe was ending that cycle.

Folding his arms, Rafe turned around. Annie needed a break from the clinic—from him—but Jenn wasn't on her way. The clinic needed two physicians. This was Annie's sanctuary, and Rafe would take care of it until she came home.

And if she sent him on his way when she returned—

His heart clenched. If Annie asked him to leave, he would go—but not until he'd told her how much he loved her. She deserved to know that someone loved *Annie*—not Charlotte Greene or her past.

Liam raised an eyebrow as the engine of Jack's plane roared to life outside. "I could make you go."

Rafe cocked his head. "Maybe—but I'm banking on you giving me a chance."

"Why should I?" Liam scoffed.

Pulling at the collar of his shirt, Rafe looked at the ceiling. "I don't have a good reason. But I love Annie. I believe she loves me too. I can't prove that to her if I run now."

Running a hand through his hair, Liam shrugged. "She might kill me for not forcing you to get on that plane."

"She might." Rafe nodded.

He doubted it. Annie was too kind and generous to stay mad at Liam. Rafe wasn't sure how long it would take him to earn back her trust, but he was ready to wait.

"Let me try to make this right."

The shrill ring of the phone interrupted him. "Blue Ash Clinic." Rafe rolled his eyes as another reporter launched into her spiel. "No comment."

Reporters were clogging the line. What if there was an emergency—?

"How many in the town know your cell number?"

Liam's head rocked back. "Why?"

"We need a line for people to call if there's an emergency."

He waited for Liam to argue, but he shook his head as he lifted his phone.

"Mom? Activate the town call chain. If anyone wants to reach the clinic they need to call my cell or—" Liam snapped his fingers and motioned for Rafe to write his own mobile number down, then read it to Helen. "That's Rafe's cell."

Liam was quiet for several minutes. Rafe didn't want to know what Helen thought of him.

Finally, Liam interrupted his mother. "Well, I need a physician here until Annie is healed and he's staying."

Rafe smiled. It wasn't a ringing endorsement, but it was a start.

Liam turned to him. "All right—why don't you walk me through the clinic's records for the past few weeks? Assuming Annie doesn't flay me for letting you stay, I'm going to need to know what's going on with our patients."

Our. The subtle inclusion warmed Rafe's heart. This was home—now he just had to convince Annie that her attention was all he needed to feel whole.

* * *

The cold water of the shower beat across her back, but Annie couldn't find the strength to turn the faucets off. Laying her head against the wall, she let her tears fall. What did it matter if goose bumps rose along her skin or if her cheeks were blotchy from the cold and her tears? If she could slide down the drain with the water she'd gladly disappear.

When her tear ducts had finally emptied, Annie wrapped a warm towel around herself and sat on the floor. Her body was heavy.

If she left Liam's cabin now would Rafe still be at the clinic? Did it matter if he was?

She choked out another sob. Why would Rafe stay?

For me?

Except it wasn't Annie he wanted—not really.

She wanted to bang the questions out of her head but aggravating her concussion wouldn't help anyone.

Sighing, she looked up. Drops of water clung to the popcorn ceiling. "I should have gotten out when the water slipped from cool to freezing," she said aloud. Pressing her palms to her eyelids, she sighed as the pressure relieved a bit of her headache. "And now I'm talking to my-self—about water!"

Swallowing, she closed her eyes. More tears leaked down her cheeks. Why had Rafe needed her interview for the promotion? He was the best doctor on the show, he drew the most viewers—it would have been his without her.

Annie wanted to believe that he hadn't used her. If *CelebNews* had plastered any other picture on that page…

She put her fist to her mouth, but it didn't stop her sobs from echoing against the bathroom tile.

Forcing herself to stand, she secured the towel around herself and stared at the fogged mirror. Raising a hand, she swiped at it until her face stared back at her. Her eyes were puffy, and her face was still bruised, but Rafe's words hung around her heart.

When she looked in the mirror what did she see?

A mess.

She covered her lips as hysterical laughter escaped her mouth. She was a soggy, pathetic, freckled mess. She was pretty sure any dictionary could use a picture of her rather than words and people would instantly understand what *pathetic* meant.

"I see me."

The phrase echoed in the small bathroom as Annie tried to make herself believe it.

"I see *me*."

A tear ran down her cheek. It was Charlotte Greene staring back at her, and Annie stamped her foot and let out a scream.

"Go away!"

Her image mocked her.

"I'm Dr. Annie Masters."

How long was she going to let her past haunt her?

"I'm Dr. Annie Masters!"

Shaking her head, Annie turned her back on the mirror. Arguing with herself wasn't going to change anything.

She tried to rub some heat into her body as she pulled on a sweater and headed into the kitchen. Rafe's journal sat on the counter. She'd meant to hand it back to him.

Ignoring the black leather, Annie grabbed a mug and made a cup of tea. *She was not going to read Rafe's journal.*

Opening a drawer, Annie threw the journal into it. Slamming the drawer shut gave her a moment of satisfaction before her stomach dropped.

Rafe was gone—or would be soon.

Her head ached, her heart wept and Annie didn't know what to do.

Downing two headache tablets, Annie walked to the living room. Falling into the couch, she stared at the picture of Blake on Liam's mantel. He was wearing his Army fatigues and smiling.

Annie wrapped her hands around the mug, willing the heat from the tea to touch her soul. She'd given her life to make Blake's dream come true.

Would she have founded a clinic in LA if he'd asked?

No.

The question and her mind's immediate answer tore through her. She'd made Blake's dream come true because she loved him, but Blue Ash had given her the privacy she craved. It had let her hide.

Blake had called her brave once. Told her she could do anything. What would he think of her now?

Annie closed her eyes. She'd been so lost when he'd died. She had lived for the clinic—hadn't let anything else touch her heart—until Rafe had wandered through her door.

Blake would be so proud of the clinic—but

he wouldn't approve of her hiding here. He'd be furious that she wasn't taking vacations. Livid that she had used his dream as a reason to avoid going back to LA.

Annie's mind raced.

What if Rafe hadn't used her? What if he wanted all of her? Past, present and future?

Rubbing the pulled skin along her thumb, Annie stared at the light snow drifting across the edge of Liam's picture window.

She couldn't lose someone again.

Annie shook as she sobbed. Her heart was already broken. She'd lost Rafe. She'd walked away from him.

She pulled her knees up to her chest.

When Blake had died, she hadn't been able to follow him—but she could go after Rafe.

She stood and walked back to the kitchen. Her palms itched as she pulled Rafe's journal from the drawer.

What did he want her to see?

Only one way to find out.

Annie stared at the binding on the journal. What if she opened it and found out it was Charlotte he needed?

Her brain screamed as her heart burst.

Charlotte. She was *not* going to let Charlotte Greene stop her from finding out what Rafe wanted her to know. Her character was a part of her, but it was a small part. She refused to live in her shadow anymore—no matter what was in Rafe's journal.

Running her fingers along the journal's binding, she inhaled and broke open the cover. The first page was ripped out, and the next three pages were grocery lists and workout schedules. Frowning, she riffled through the following pages. A torn page slipped to the ground. It had been crumpled and then smoothed out.

Her heart broke as she looked at the lines.

Goals:
Get into med school
Secure residency position
Complete residence
Move out of studio apartment
Visit all fifty states
~~Get permanent position on Dr. Dave~~
~~Find Mom~~
~~Meet Mom~~
Tell Annie you love her
Buy shoes that work for the Arctic
Move to Alaska

Her heart wanted to sing, but Annie wasn't going to celebrate yet. This page had been ripped out. What if there was another list that had all the ways he could use Annie's old fame to advance his position?

Flipping through the well-used journal, Annie held her breath. Rafe might have ripped those pages out before handing her the journal, but Annie doubted it. He wanted to let her see what he'd been thinking. Let her know his hopes and dreams.

A list of the interview ideas they'd worked on that morning appeared. She'd been so happy as she'd sat beside Rafe. Ink stained through the next page, and she couldn't make out some of the words. Whatever this list was, Rafe had clearly worked hard on it.

Ways to tell Annie I love her:
Just say it
Dinner
Roses
Dinner with roses
Donuts!

Tears showered her cheeks. He'd been hiding surprises and she had told him to leave. Accused him of using her when she knew how much that accusation would cripple him.

But it didn't matter what these pages said if Rafe was gone.

Rafe loved her.

There had to be an explanation for the *Celeb-News* story, and only Rafe could give her that answer.

Annie sucked in a breath. Liam was in town and would run the clinic for a few days without her. Her fingers hovered over Rafe's list. She needed to pick up a few things and pack. If Rafe was in LA, then that was where she needed to be too.

Annie yawned as she made her way up the clinic's steps. In order to avoid the questioning eyes of the people of Blue Ash and aggravating her concussion, Annie had begged Holly to run a few errands for her. Holly hadn't agreed until Annie had told her about Rafe's lists. However, she'd needed to wait until the bakery closed. Then a car accident on the highway had derailed her friend's quick return.

But now Annie had everything she needed to head to California, and she'd promised Holly a nice souvenir for all her trouble.

Lugging her bags up the stairs, Annie's heart clenched at the thought of sleeping without Rafe. She'd grown accustomed to his warm weight beside her, his light breath on her neck…

If all her flights were on time she'd be in his arms the day after tomorrow. *Too long...*

Dropping the bags in the kitchen, Annie stumbled through to the living room. She didn't want to risk waking Liam. He'd have questions, and she was too exhausted to address any of them.

Her toe landed against something hard, and Annie let out a screech as she tumbled forward. Strong arms grabbed her before she hit the floor.

"Annie?" Rafe's voice was groggy with sleep as his hands ran over her. *"Annie?"*

He blinked as she flipped on the light. "What are you doing on the floor?" *What was he doing still in Blue Ash?*

That question stayed buried as she ran her fingers over his arms. He was here—he was still here.

"Sleeping."

Rafe smiled at her. This wasn't the frantic desire of his subconscious. Annie was here. *She was here.*

"Why are you sleeping on the floor?"

Her cheeks flushed as she stared at him.

"Wasn't sure you wanted me in our bed."

Rafe rubbed his hands across his face as he drank her in. Reaching a finger out, he pushed a loose curl away from her cheek, grateful that she didn't pull away.

"What are you still doing here, Rafe? Your show—"

"Doesn't matter," he interrupted. "This clinic needs more than one physician. I couldn't leave it—couldn't leave *you*."

"I am so sorry, Rafe. I'm glad you didn't leave. I should have chosen you—not run." Annie hiccupped as she pressed her lips to his cheek. Her shoulders shook as she laid her head against him. "Can you forgive me?"

Rafe wrapped his arms around her. She was here. Annie—*his Annie*—was home with him.

"Forgive you? I'm the one that kept major secrets and took a picture that landed on the front page of a tabloid."

Her lips stole the apology tumbling from his. The world shifted and nothing else mattered as she melted against him. Annie was here; she was choosing him. Time slowed as her fingers pulled against his neck, demanding he deepen the kiss.

"I love you." Rafe pulled her into his lap. "I just need you to know that before anything else. I should have said it after the carnival, but I was hiding so many things."

He brushed his lips against her cheek. "I didn't tell you about the interview because I thought you'd agree to help. You're too sweet, and I didn't want to take advantage of your good nature. Figured if you didn't know I could tell Dave you hadn't agreed. I should have just told you everything."

Annie placed her arms around his waist. "You were trying to protect me."

Rafe pressed his head against hers. "I feared you'd hate me if you thought I was trying to find a way to use an interview with you to get the promotion. My dad used my mom for so many things, and I—" Rafe pressed his lips together. "I never want you to feel I used you."

"I was so afraid of my past that you didn't feel you could be honest with me." Annie laid her head against his shoulder. "I'm so much more than my character, but Charlotte is a part of me. I can't keep running from her. You made me see that."

She was grinning. He'd never seen her smile

when the name Charlotte crossed her lips. He thought his world might explode.

Inhaling, Rafe pushed away his fear. "I love you."

He just needed to repeat those words.

"I love you. So, what if we put the past behind us and focus on the future?"

He didn't care about the late hour as Annie's smile radiated through him.

"I'm still under contract through the end of the year. I need to do that final interview and the Thanksgiving and Christmas shows. I don't know if I can be here this winter."

Annie laid a finger across his lips. "I want you here this winter, Rafe Bradstone, but I don't want you to give up all of the spotlight."

"Annie—" He gripped her fingers.

She ignored his attempt to interrupt. "What if the Christmas and Thanksgiving episodes were pre-recorded and shot at our clinic?"

Our—he loved that word. But...

"Dave likes the Thanksgiving show to be live. I'm not sure he'll go for it."

"Even if I'm the other host?"

Annie let out a whoop as Rafe picked her up.

"You'd co-host so I could stay here for the winter?" Rafe's heart felt as if it would burst as she held onto him.

Annie nodded. "If you're by my side I can step in front of any camera."

"I love you." Rafe smiled. "We'll do the shows and then we can tell Hollywood so long."

"No." Annie laid her hand on his chin. "I think we should do a few shows a year—in the summer, when it's easy for me to get replacements for us here."

"Us?" Rafe's fingers shook as he traced her jaw. "You'd come to LA with me."

"I'll go anywhere with you." Her fingers were soft as they ran along his unshaved cheek. "I'll bet Dr. Dave is willing to settle for a part-time Dr. Bradstone. But I'm not—so we spend most of the year in our clinic and a month in LA. We're a package deal now."

"I love you," Rafe said again. No other words seemed adequate.

Grabbing his hand, Annie led him to the kitchen. Her cheeks were flushed and her breath tightened as she stepped away. Opening a bag, she tossed him his journal before grabbing a pen.

"I think there's an item you need to check off."

Running his hand along the spine, Rafe smiled

again. "Actually, I think there are a few items I can mark off."

"True." Annie giggled as she handed him a bag. "But this one is very important."

Rafe raised an eyebrow. "What's this?"

"Only one way to find out." Annie crossed her arms. "Open it!"

His breath caught as he stared into the bag. Slowly, he lifted out a heavy navy-blue boot. "You got me—" His voice cracked.

Knocking her hip against his, Annie lifted the other. "These are rated to minus forty degrees Fahrenheit. Can't have Dr. Bradstone losing any toes! Welcome home, Rafe."

Home. The precious word rumbled through his soul.

"Thank you." Rafe kissed the top of her head. "These are perfect. However, if it's negative forty outside, I have every intention of curling up next to you beside a warm fire—not stomping around in the snow."

"I think we can arrange that." Annie smiled.

"Marry me?"

The words slipped into the quiet kitchen. He should have planned it out. Given her a fancy dinner, flowers or donuts—something. But Rafe couldn't wait.

"Yes!" Annie leapt into his arms.

Annie had chosen *him*—all of him.

Dr. Rafe Bradstone was finally home.

EPILOGUE

"IS DADDY GOING to be done soon?"

Lilah pulled at Annie's dress and raised her arms. Lifting her daughter was getting more difficult these days.

Annie looked at the program set, where Rafe was confidently talking to a surgeon about a new hand reconstruction technique. Most of the segment would be cut—if not all of it. It was interesting to doctors, and some researchers, but the average daytime television viewer would have tuned to a new show within the first three minutes.

"If he can stop geeking out with Dr. Jameson, he'll be done soon."

Lilah frowned. Then the three-year-old laid her head against Annie's shoulder before letting out a squeal. "The baby kicked me again!"

Setting her daughter down, Annie caught Rafe's eye. He smiled when he saw her motion for him to move on. If he didn't want a screaming toddler to interrupt Dr. Dave's taping, it was time to go.

Annie had appeared in a few episodes but returning to show business held no appeal for her. Rafe still loved it, though. Usually Lilah and Annie stayed far away from the set, but they were supposed to head to the airport as soon as this was over. She had every intention of being back in Blue Ash by tomorrow afternoon—if her husband would wrap up his showboating.

Rafe rushed over as soon as the segment ended. "Is everything okay?"

Placing a kiss on his lips, Annie smiled. "Yep, but your daughter is ready to go." Leaning up, she nipped the bottom of his ear, enjoying the way he shuddered and pulled her close. "And your wife is too."

"In a rush to get back to the snow?" Rafe laughed as he lifted Lilah.

"The baby kicked me!" Their daughter's bottom lip stuck out as she repeated her complaint to her father.

Annie covered her mouth and looked away. If Lilah saw her giggle, she'd pout the whole way to the airport.

"He does that to me too," Rafe murmured as he led his small family out of the studio.

"Really?"

"Yes—when your mother snuggles up next to me, your brother kicks quite hard. But so did you."

Rafe winked at Annie as he buckled their daughter into the car. He laid a kiss on Lilah's head before sliding into the driver's seat.

"Dave wants to know if you'll let him do a spring segment at the clinic. He wants a follow-up about its growth over the last four years."

Annie leaned over, capturing her husband's mouth. "I have all winter to decide. Do you have your boots?"

Rafe grabbed the boots she'd gotten him all those years ago and smiled. "Always."

Annie sighed as his lips met hers. "I love you. Let's go home."

* * * * *

LET'S TALK

For exclusive extracts, competitions
and special offers, find us online:

- facebook.com/millsandboon
- @millsandboonuk
- @millsandboon

Or get in touch on 0844 844 1351*

For all the latest titles coming soon,
visit millsandboon.co.uk/nextmonth

*Calls cost 7p per minute plus your phone company's price per
minute access charge